P9-CDV-215

I don't know these dances! And as soon as the next dance starts, I'm going to be standing here alone while Emily dashes off to dance with Trent. It's like my worst nightmare, come to life.

Turns out 1815 isn't so different from the twenty-first century, because this is *exactly* what would happen if I were back home.

Why did I think it would change? Flying thousands of miles to Europe didn't change my fate. Traveling two hundred years, it seems, didn't either.

PRADA&
PREJUDICE

· MANDY HUBBARD ·

NEW HANOVER COUNTY
PUBLIC LIBRARY
201 CHESTNUT STREET
WILMINGTON, NC 28401

Prada and Prejudice

RAZORBILL

Published by the Penguin Group
Penguin Young Readers Group
345 Hudson Street, New York, New York 10014, U.S.A.
Penguin Group (USA) Inc., 375 Hudson Street, New York, New York 10014, U.S.A.
Penguin Group (Canada), 90 Eglinton Avenue East, Suite 700, Toronto, Ontario,
Canada M4P 2Y3 (a division of Pearson Penguin Canada Inc.)
Penguin Books Ltd, 80 Strand, London WC2R 0RL, England
Penguin Ireland, 25 St Stephen's Green, Dublin 2, Ireland
(a division of Penguin Books Ltd)
Penguin Group (Australia), 250 Camberwell Road, Camberwell, Victoria 3124,
Australia (a division of Pearson Australia Group Pty Ltd)
Penguin Books India Pvt Ltd, 11 Community Centre, Panchsheel Park, New Delhi—
110 017, India
Penguin Group (NZ), 67 Apollo Drive, Rosedale, North Shore 0632, New Zealand
(a division of Pearson New Zealand Ltd.)

Penguin Books (South Africa) (Pty) Ltd, 24 Sturdee Avenue, Rosebank,
Johannesburg 2196, South Africa

Penguin Books Ltd, Registered Offices: 80 Strand, London WC2R 0RL, England

10 9 8 7 6 5 4 3 2 1

Copyright © 2009 Mandy Hubbard

All rights reserved

Library of Congress Cataloging-in-Publication Data

Hubbard, Amanda
    Prada and prejudice / by Amanda Hubbard
        p. cm.
    Summary: During a school trip to England, fifteen-year-old Callie buys a pair of Prada
shoes in an effort to impress the popular girls, a scheme that backfires and sends Callie
back to 1815.
    ISBN: 9781595142603

1. Time travel--Fiction. 2. Self-confidence—Fiction. 3. England—Social life and
customs—19th century—Fiction.

PZ7.H856676 Pr 2009

[E] 22 Printed in the United States of America

The scanning, uploading and distribution of this book via the Internet or via any
other means without the permission of the publisher is illegal and punishable by law.
Please purchase only authorized electronic editions, and do not participate in or
encourage electronic piracy of copyrighted materials. Your support of the author's rights is
appreciated.

The publisher does not have any control over and does not assume any
responsibility for author or third-party websites or their content.

PRADA&
PREJUDICE

For my husband,
just because I love you.

1

It is a truth, universally acknowledged, that a teen girl on a class trip to England should be having the time of her life.

At least, that's what I thought. Instead I'm miserable. It took me two weeks to convince my mom I was responsible enough to go on this trip instead of staying with my dad for the rest of the summer, eight days to rush-order a passport, and precisely twenty-four hours to regret it. It's my first full day in London and instead of seeing Buckingham Palace or Big Ben or the Thames, I'm sitting in Belgaro's café inside my hotel, wishing someone, *anyone*, would give me the time of day.

The point of this trip was to tour all of London's historically significant sights as a precursor to European history. Sophomore year starts next month, and it's supposed to be the *Year We Pad our College Applications*. At least, that's what the pamphlets said.

Last year, I never would have felt this desperate. My best friend Katie and I never wanted to be one of the in-crowd zombies. In fact, we made a sport of heckling the A-list. When the yearbooks came out last spring, we drew mustaches on the popular girls and wrote little quotes of the stupid things they'd said in class.

And then Katie moved away. Without her around, it's nearly impossible to convince myself that I'm happy on the D-list. How can I be? I'm the only one *on* the D-list.

It all started when I called Katie during lunch, two days after she moved. It's probably pathetic to admit it, but I had started eating my lunch in the bathroom. I was miserable, and I needed my friend's support.

So there I was, blabbing away on my cell phone in the corner stall. I had no idea Trisha Marks (cough-SNOB-cough-cough) had walked in. She overheard the whole thing—even the part where I said cheerleaders were modern day courtesans. As you can imagine, it didn't go over so well. At least, not once Trisha looked up the definition of *courtesan* on her handy-dandy iPhone.

Now I'm hated by pretty much every pom-pom-wielding airhead at my high school.

I look up when the door chimes, and to my horror see three of my classmates stride into the room. Angela, the lanky blonde, has no less than three bags with cute little rope handles, *Chanel, Gucci,* and *Armani* proudly emblazoned across each one. Summer, her petite best friend, walks quietly in her shadow, a *Juicy* bag in hand, her dark wavy hair cascading down her shoulders. Mindy walks beside them, looking like the normal American teen she is: her messy brown hair is in a bun, and she's wearing a lace-embellished pink tank top and destroyed denim jeans. The three of them laugh at something I can't hear.

Basically, they look like they're having the trip I dreamed of. The three girls might not *be* the A-list, but they're certainly *on* it. And since Angela Marks is Trisha-the-demon-cheerleader's little sister, she's sworn in blood to defend her honor. Or, you know, give me the evil eye and ditch me, even though we're assigned travel-buddies. It's her fault I can't leave the hotel without breaking Mrs. Bentley's golden rule: Safety in pairs. Never go anywhere alone. Blah, Blah, Blah.

And now they'll see me wallowing in misery like a total loser. I shrink back in the leather booth, hoping the big leafy palm next to the table is enough to obscure my face. They *cannot* know I'm sitting here, two empty glasses of Coke next to me, like I've been here all day. Because the truth is, I *have* been here all day.

The group activities won't start until the day after tomorrow. We'll be visiting museums and palaces and going on double-decker bus tours. I can't decide if things will improve then, or just get worse. Sometimes I feel more alone when I'm surrounded by my classmates than I do when I'm actually by myself.

Why did I think this trip was going to be different?

It was supposed to be my chance to change everything. I guess I thought if we were thousands of miles from home, I'd be just as far from my old reputation. I was wrong.

For the record, I don't think it's humanly possible for me

to be friends with Angela. She definitely shares Trisha's gene pool, if you know what I mean—all the way down to the sneer she makes every time someone annoys her. But Mindy is usually in a bunch of honors classes with me, and last year sometimes we'd end up as lab partners in Chem. Maybe if I was a little more outgoing, Mindy and I would be friends by now.

She seems cool, I think, as I watch her roll her eyes at Summer when Angela's not looking. If I'd been assigned as *her* buddy for this trip, she wouldn't have ditched me. I just have to get Angela to begrudgingly accept my presence, and then maybe we could all hang out as a foursome. If I'm lucky, maybe we can switch buddies entirely.

The trio of girls set their shopping bags in a heap on the booth next to mine, oblivious to my presence behind the leafy palm. I can't see what they're doing, but I imagine Angela is picking up the menu and trying to decide between the spinach salad with no dressing or a glass of water. I'm pretty sure she's anorexic, which is easier to handle than the idea that she's naturally perfect. I mean, really—her collarbone could cut glass.

"So, should I wear this red one, which shows more cleavage, or my sparkly yellow tube top tonight?" Summer asks. She must be rifling through a bag, because all I can hear is crinkling plastic.

"Yellow tank. Definitely. It's more clubby," Angela says. "But what shoes can you wear with it?"

Seriously—clubby? Figures they're going to break all the

rules and hit a club. I never would have the guts to do something cool like that. All I have on my schedule is an in-room movie rental, which is sounding more pitiful by the minute.

Summer sighs, this great melodramatic heave that makes it seem like she's just found out she flunked sophomore year before it even started. I picture her frowning her big pouty lips and wrinkling a perfectly groomed brow. "I dunno. I swear I packed my black Guccis, but they weren't in my bag."

"Those aren't Guccis. They're knockoffs," Angela says in a sharp voice.

Oh, snap. I look down at my Old Navy flip-flops poking out from under the table, and then slide them further underneath me.

"So?" Summer says, her voice rising an octave. "Do they look that bad?"

Mindy says, "Well, it's not like guys can tell the difference."

Angela makes a growling sound. Her minions have spoken back, so she must be trying to assert her dominance. I don't speak *Angela*, so I can't know for sure. I imagine right now she's flipping her platinum blonde hair over her shoulder while rolling her eyes. "Well, *I* can. Did you see that girl at the coffee stand this morning? She was wearing fake Pradas. I mean, seriously. Does she really think she's fooling someone?"

Yeah. Angela is seriously the most stereotypical Valley Girl I've ever met. She's a walking cliché. It doesn't stop people from worshipping her, though. With flawless skin, sparkling blue eyes, and the bounciest hair I've ever seen, I can't really blame them.

Now I imagine Mindy rolling her eyes, wishing they were having a more intelligent conversation. The kind she could have with me, for instance. We could be strolling up and down the fancy walkways and admiring English architecture while we debate the theory of evolution. Or at least how much we hate Mr. Thomason, our Honors Chemistry teacher from freshman year. During our first lab together, I almost burned off my hair with a Bunsen burner and all I got from him was a lecture in front of the entire class. The man has no sympathy.

"Fine. Let's go find a good pair of heels after lunch," Summer says. "But you have to help me with the conversion rate. I think I might have overspent already."

"Like I can figure it out either. I'm just charging everything," Angela says. Rumor has it Angela comes equipped with a black, limitless AmEx card.

"I'll help you," Mindy says. "It's pretty simple."

It *is* simple, but whatever. There's a reason I'll be voted "Class Brain" and Summer will get "Major Catch," and it's not because she's good at math.

"What's this place called, anyway?" Summer asks.

"I don't know. It's at the end of Sloane Street, where it dead-ends at Hyde Park or something. We're supposed to meet up with the guys at the backdoor at nine," Angela says.

I can't believe this. They're crashing a nightclub while I'm stuck in the room. This isn't fair. Why can't I go too?

The waitress strolls up to take their order (Angela shocks me by ordering a cheeseburger), and I develop a game plan as

I nervously jiggle a spare straw between my thumb and index finger. I'll saunter slowly by, and then when I look over and see Mindy, I'll act surprised. Then I'll ask her if she's gotten any reading done on Mr. Brown's summer reading list. If at all possible, I'll segue into how boring London has been so far, and maybe they'll invite me out with them. My plan is flawless.

My stomach is already twisting and flopping around in protest, but my mind is made up. I have to get this over with. I fish my mango lip gloss out of the pocket of my Levis and smear it on, and then smooth over my slightly frizzed-out blonde hair.

No time like the present. I slide quickly out of the leather booth and am almost to my feet when someone slams into me from behind.

Oomph. I'm knocked to my knees, but I manage to catch myself before face planting.

That's when I feel a chill seeping through my shirt, spreading so my entire back is covered in icy-coldness, and goose bumps pop up all over my arms. I twist my head and see a woman holding a half empty pitcher of iced tea, a black apron tied around her waist.

"Are you okay, love? Oh blimey, you're soaked! I'm so sorry. I was just walking by and you jumped out in front of me," she says, more to herself than me. "Let me help you up."

"Uh, I'm okay, really. No biggie."

I take a deep breath and look up at the trio of girls next to me. Angela is fighting a huge grin (and losing) but Mindy is just staring, her face blank of all expression. Summer is hiding behind a menu, her face turned downward so all I can see is her highlight-streaked dark hair.

"You okay?" Mindy asks.

"Smooth move," Angela says. "Very graceful."

Summer's tiny shoulders shake with silent giggles as my face nearly bursts into flames.

"Oh. Uh, I'm fine. I'm just . . . soaked. I, uh, I'm fine. Thanks."

And then I bail. There's no way I can talk to them now. Like they're going to invite me to the club? Ha. Right. I've just confirmed the reason they don't hang out with me. God, I'm a walking disaster.

I bolt through the café's side-door and duck into the hotel lobby bathroom, the closest door to the scene of my humiliation. I go into one of the fancy pink wallpapered stalls and sit down on a toilet for a few minutes, my face buried in my hands, trying to compose myself. There's a lump in my throat, but I won't cry because it's not worth it. This kind of stuff happens to me all the time, and tomorrow it won't sting so much. I'll block it from my memory like it never happened.

My mom has always told me I have two left feet, but I think that's giving me too much credit. I'm so clumsy I deserve my own cliché. I'm sure eventually falling flat on your face will be known as "pulling a Callie Montgomery."

I get up and leave the stall, the automatic toilet flushing behind me. I shuffle to the sinks, sniffling back the last few tears that still threaten.

Once in front of the gilded mirror, I twist around to survey the damage. My white tee is totally soaked through so you can see my black bra strap. The ends of my lifeless blonde hair aren't exempt from the iced tea treatment, either. They even smell like lemon.

I sigh and grip the edges of the sink as I stare back at my reflection. It's not like I'm horrendously ugly. I'm just kind of plain. Straight, narrow nose. Average cheekbones. Dull blue eyes. Could I *be* anymore average?

It's no wonder I've never even been kissed. My lips are sort of thin. Not full and kissable like Angela's.

The door swings open and I look up to see Mindy stride in. I yank back from the mirror so she won't know I've been staring at myself.

She's retying the knot in her charcoal-gray shrug when she sees me, and her glossy lips part—and then freeze like that—a tiny little *o* of surprise.

I drop my hands to my sides and try to ignore the prickling feeling of the wet shirt glued to my back.

"Oh," she says, and then stops at the door, halfway into the bathroom and halfway out, like she might get bubonic plague from me if she gets too close.

"Hey," I say. My hands are suddenly in need of a good washing, so I stare at the soap dispenser as I pump it five times, filling my palm with pink suds. I'm overly aware of her presence in my peripheral vision, and have to force my eyes to remain on the ultraimportant task of personal hygiene. Why is she staring at me like that?

Mindy finally walks into the bathroom stall as I switch the faucet off and reach for a few paper towels. I use them slowly, one square at a time, until she comes back out.

I toss the paper towels and pretend to fix a few strands of hair as she walks toward the sinks. She stops halfway there.

"Oh, um, Callie?"

I perk up and turn to look at her. She's smiling at me.

This is *it!* My ticket out of the hotel.

"Um, I just wanted to, well—" she pauses for a second.

My heart is going crazy. I knew Mindy would come through if I gave her the chance. I just know we'd click if I could stop acting like a freak for more than five minutes.

She clears her throat. "You have toilet paper stuck to your shoe."

2

"Huh?" I look down at my flip-flops and the giant chunk of toilet paper trailing off the toe of one of them. "Oh. Uh, thanks."

I reach down, yank off the T.P., and then rush for the door without another word.

I make it out the front of the hotel before I even know what I'm doing. I haven't had the guts to leave without a "buddy" ever since the big lecture from Mrs. Bentley yesterday when we arrived. She swore if she caught any of us out alone she'd send us home.

But if I want to get back to my room, I have to walk right through the café again, my flip-flops slapping against my feet to announce my arrival. I'd have to walk past Angela and her sneer and Summer and her giggles.

I can't take any more of them right now. I have to get away and clear my head and figure out how I'm going to get through this trip.

I slow down when I realize I've gone several blocks on Sloane Street without noticing. Our fancy five-star hotel is situated in the best shopping district in London, or at least that's what Angela talked about the whole flight here.

Not that she was talking to me, of course. She was sitting between Summer and Mindy, in the row in front of me. I got a window seat next to an elderly man who snored the whole flight. Even though I pretended to be reading, I eavesdropped on them the whole time. I think Angela was listing the designers in alphabetical order; I got lost after Armani, Burberry, Chanel, Coach, and Dior.

I must be on the right track, because the waif-thin girls walking past me look like models, and I think I just saw the third foreign sports car in as many minutes.

Crazy. I definitely don't see *that* every day. Our little country town is more likely to have jacked-up trucks and a Target than Ferraris and a Louis Vuitton shop.

The architecture here is gorgeous: all sorts of brick buildings, elaborate archways, stone carvings, open-air cafés, glossy store fronts . . . everything is just so *English* I feel a little sophisticated and chic just walking down this street, like I should be eating a croissant or debating the finer sides of Chaucer or something.

Maybe if I soak up a little of this. . . *aura*, I can act a little less classic Callie and figure out a plan to get to the club tonight.

Hyde Park and Sloane Street. That's where the club is. Maybe I can pick up some cute clothes and then go scope it out and it won't seem so intimidating. Maybe I can get the nerve to crash later. Mindy is pretty nice, after all. She could be cool with it. If I look cute and act normal, they'll get over their idea that I'm deadweight.

Still deep in thought, I pass a window filled with mannequins. One of them has a baby blue cami just like the pink one Mindy was wearing.

Yes, this could work.

Step 1: Retail Therapy.

Two hours later, my arms and feet are killing me. I'm still not sure what look I'm going for, but if I can't decide on something from the two-hundred dollars—er, *pounds*—worth of clothes I've bought so far, I'm hopeless. The thing is, I don't want to seem like I'm trying too hard but I don't want to dress like a total scrub either. I have to look killer tonight. Pulled off correctly, it will reverse my fate, and the rest of my European vacation will be spent with Mindy, having real fun.

I'm just about to turn around and head back to the hotel when I see it: a five-story brick building with huge bay windows on every floor. Fluted white casings frame the entry. At the street level is a wall of glass, polished to such a shine I can see my own reflection staring back at me.

And hanging over my head, in shockingly simple block letters, is a single word: *PRADA*.

I stare at the storefront with Angela's words ringing in my head. She knows shoes. She knows fakes. And she knows the real thing when she sees it. What if I bought a pair of true Prada shoes and wore them to the club? Would she admire them? Would she at least say something and break the ice, and then I could say something brilliant back, and she'd forget that she never invited me out in the first place?

Desperate times call for desperate measures. The desperate measure in this case being my Mom's credit card, which was given to me with a stern warning about "emergency usage only." In my book, this qualifies as an emergency. After all, I'm about to have a life-changing night.

Still outside, I peer farther into the store. There's a banner announcing the arrival of the summer collection, and a dozen or so pairs of heels on little acrylic perches. I spot a pair of lavender platform pumps that makes my heart jump—the heel is painted to look like little flowers. But then I think about what Angela would say, and I realize they're too showy. That's when I see them: a pair of shiny red patent leather pumps with sky-high heels and a cute buckle detail. They're totally classic, and yet there's no way anyone could mistake them for another brand. My mind made up, I shove open the door and step inside. I'm not even going to try them on; they're mine.

As it turns out, I probably should have tried them on because they definitely feel too big, now that I'm actually standing in them. But I'm sure I can figure out a way to stuff some tissue in the front. It'll be fine. I just have to get back to the hotel.

Which is, unfortunately, at least a mile away, back by the Chelsea Bridge and the Thames.

I stand precariously in the tallest heels I've ever worn,

determined to make it back to my room. The good thing is that by the time I get there, they'll have lost a little bit of their brand-new look, and then when Angela compliments me on them, I can be all, "Oh, these old things?"

I take a few clumsy steps, and that's when it happens: the heel snags a grate, my ankle twists, and I'm free falling. My breath catches in my throat because I know whatever happens next is going to hurt. The cement is rushing up at me so fast I can't even protect my head. The last thing I see is a well-dressed guy with salt-and-pepper hair staring at me with wide eyes as my arms fly out like chicken wings.

Pain screams in my temple as I slam to the pavement, and then the world goes black.

3

There's a pounding inside my skull, like a jackhammer is drilling out my eyeballs. Nausea wells up, but I sit still for a few long moments, keeping my eyes closed until it abates, and the pounding in my head fades to a drumbeat in the background.

I ease one eye open, waiting for the pounding to resume, but it doesn't. I open my other eye, but the headache is gone. Whew.

Once my eyes are open, however, a new problem presents itself: I'm sitting in dirt. Damp, mucky dirt. My left hand, the one I'm leaning on, is sinking in it. I snap my head upward.

My pulse quickens and a scream catches in my throat.

I'm surrounded by trees. And not a few trees, like I might have been moved from the sidewalk to a nearby park—this is big enough to be a national forest. The sun is setting, and all I can see are tree trunks and shadows and more dirt. Some birds have the nerve to chirp, like this is just another day in their lives.

This makes no sense. None at all.

My hand shakes as I reach up to rub my eyes, sure I'm hallucinating. When I open them again, nothing has changed.

Oh God, oh God, oh God. This is wrong. All wrong.

I look around, forcing myself to take several long, slow breaths.

Do. Not. Panic.

There has to be a simple explanation for this.

My shopping bags are gone. All three of them. Have I been robbed? My purse is still gripped tightly in my hand, and a quick glance tells me the contents are still intact. So where's the rest of my stuff? I glance down at my feet and am relieved to see my four-hundred-dollar Prada shoes. Whew.

I pull my knees up to my chest and rest my forehead on them. My left temple is tender and sore where it hit the concrete.

I chew on my lip and look around again. What on earth is going on?

I bought these shoes. Took a few steps. Fell down.

And now I'm . . . in the middle of nowhere?

This can't be right. I don't remember seeing any trees like this. Maybe they were behind the shops. Maybe someone moved me out of the way of traffic.

But as I look in each direction, all I see are more trees. There must be hundreds. No, thousands. The more I see, the more I want to take off running. What the heck is going on? How is it that I smack my head in the middle of London and wake up in the forest?

Something howls in the distance, and I scramble to my feet. Oh God. Does England have wolves? Maybe it was just a dog. But it sounded huge. Really, really huge.

I start walking briskly in the opposite direction, my heels sinking in the dirt. I have to hold my arms out to balance myself; it feels like I'm walking in quick sand. It is going to take forever to get anywhere. And the sun is already falling in the sky. That's bad. That's really bad. I don't want to be out here in the dark.

I take a deep breath, trying to calm my heart, which has gone crazy in my chest. This is the kind of bizarre thing that happens on the news. Not to me.

I trip on some tree roots and land on my knees, the mud quickly seeping through my jeans. Tears spring to my eyes as I scramble back to my feet. This is marvelous. Exactly how I wanted to spend my evening. I should be at a party, dancing and exchanging witty barbs with Angela and Mindy. But no, I'm walking around in England's National Forest. Alone. As darkness falls.

I still don't get it. Why am I here?

What if I'm not even walking in a straight line? I could be circling! I could be out here forever!

It's cold and way too silent. The canopy of the forest is blocking most of the remaining light, making it way too dark for my comfort. Did something just move? No, that was just a leaf falling. I'm being paranoid.

Ten minutes of walking, cursing England and everything in it, and I hear something. It's like a roaring, almost like a train, except not quite as loud. And then there's a horse whinny. What the heck? That can't be good.

I duck behind a giant oak tree, well obscured by the wide trunk, and watch. *Please* don't be an ax murderer.

A carriage appears, pulled by four gray horses. Have I woken up in some kind of fairy tale? I stare as the wheels roll by and the ground shakes beneath my feet. The thundering noise quiets as the carriage rolls away, and I realize maybe I should have asked for help.

Maybe they were nice people and they could have helped me.

A sinking feeling comes over me. What if I'm really *really* far away? What if I'm lost forever? They could find my body or something, deep in the woods. And they won't know what happened to me. Because *I* don't know what happened to me.

This is so not good. So *not* good.

I have no choice. I have to keep walking. I can't see any sign of civilization, but I can't be that far from the hotel. Or at least a house and someone with a phone. I can call Mrs. Bentley, but how am I going to explain this? She doesn't want us leaving the hotel unaccompanied, and I inexplicably end up lost in the woods? She's not going to buy that.

At least the carriage has shown me the road paralleling the path I'm walking, so I move over fifty feet and use that instead. It's only moderately better than the trees—there are deep ruts on both sides of the road, and no gravel, just mud and compact dirt. Thankfully, my heels don't sink here, so I can walk faster. The light is a little better too, so at least I'm not tripping as much.

It's incredibly silent. The only sound is my heels scraping the road, a steady noise that seems far too loud. The sun hasn't disappeared yet, but the moon is rising behind me and the stars are already glittering. The light glints across the scattered mud puddles. I try not to notice that there seem to be so many more stars than there were last night.

I walk until the sun is just a sliver on the horizon, wishing I had stopped the carriage and asked for help. My toes are blistered and the back of my feet are raw where the heel keeps rubbing on them. My head spins.

Could this be a dream? Maybe I was knocked unconscious and I'm really sitting in a hospital bed coming up with this whole crazy story. That's plausible. Sort of.

Argh! I can't believe this. Tears spring to my eyes again, only this time, I let them roll down my cheeks. This isn't fair. I didn't do anything to deserve this. Angela should be the one showcasing her survival skills. *She* made fun of *me*. Karma is supposed to catch up with things like that, not kick me when I'm down.

Today is officially the worst day of my life. Why did I have to talk my mom into letting me go to England? She was right. I wasn't ready for a foreign country. If my mom was here right now, I'd tell her that and beg her to take me home. I'd spend the rest of the summer doing my usual stuff: movies, surfing the internet, magazines, junk food. Maybe that stuff will never make up for the things I really want, but it won't get me stuck in England's wilderness either.

There's something ahead of me. I duck behind a tree again, trying to figure out what it is. I squint. There's a glowing in the distance. Lights! I must be close to someone's house! I jump out from behind the tree and scurry toward the lights, as quickly as my blister-clad toes will let me.

My shoes must be ruined by now. Four-hundred dollars down the drain. How am I going to explain *that* one to my mom? I consider ditching the heels altogether, but being barefoot doesn't seem any better, so I keep them on.

As I get within fifty feet of the lights, I realize that they're lanterns. Real, flaming, oil-filled lanterns.

But it's a house! Or at least, I can make out a rooftop amidst the shadows.

When I reach the crest of a small hill, I'm shocked to see the house that *belongs* to the rooftop. Calling it a house seems silly. It's a *castle*. It stretches out before me, perched on a grassy knoll, two big wings on either side of the main entry. Ivy is climbing up one side, its green vines covering the east wing. The entire building is made of stone, like a castle you'd imagine in a fairy tale, and in the dusk it looks both stately and scary. I stare at it for a long moment, wondering what kind of people are inside. They must be super rich. Will they help me? Or will they think I'm some crazy runaway teen or something?

With no other choice, I limp toward the front door as the rocks transition to cobblestones. My feet are pounding and I'm shivering. It had seemed so warm earlier, but the dampness from the mud has taken all that away. In the last twenty minutes, the wind has kicked up, and it's whistling through the trees. If they don't help me . . . I can't bear to think of what I'll be faced with.

I pass a big pond with a few geese paddling merrily on its surface and make my way to the entry. The door is huge—twice as tall as it needs to be. It's big enough to be the door to the Emerald City.

I close my eyes as I knock. *You will help me. You will help me. You will help me.*

4

The door of the mansion swings open before I can even drop my fist, like someone has been standing on the other side the entire time. The elderly man staring back at me is thin and frail, with a sneer and a hard glare that makes me want to step back. My stomach twists. He doesn't look very friendly. He's dressed in a really old fashioned way, wearing a starched white shirt and black jacket, and get this—he's wearing a powdered wig like George Washington or something. He looks down at my dirty jeans and T-shirt, and then moves to shut the door in my face.

"Wait!" I say, and stick my foot into the entry. The door bounces off my aching toes and sends a wave of pain up my leg. Yes, my shoes are most definitely trashed now. "Please, I, uh, I n-need your help," I stutter. Is it crazy to even *want* help from a guy wearing a powdered wig? "I'm lost and—"

"Rebecca?" a girl's voice calls, in one of those pure, melodic British accents.

I crane my neck around the still half-closed door, hoping to catch a glimpse of whoever the girl is, but she barrels at me so quickly I barely get a glimpse of her brown hair and beautiful pale skin before she's throwing her arms around me.

"It is you!" she squeals. "I knew it must be by your American accent! We hadn't expected you for a month yet! I've only just received your last letter stating that you were soon to purchase your tickets for the sea voyage." She envelops me in a hug so tight I can't breathe. I squish against her, and I can tell she's wearing a corset underneath her old fashioned dress, because the ribbing pokes me through my T-shirt. I think she's close to my age, probably less than eighteen, but with the clothes she seems older.

The lanterns, the old-fashioned clothes, the carriage . . . the size of those trees . . . and the way the stars look . . .

No, that's crazy. England just looks a lot different from America, that's all. England probably has better environmental regulations.

I realize I'm staring at the girl when she laughs awkwardly. "It's me, Emily! It's truly been a long time, has it not? I believe we were seven when we last saw each other! Oh, how I missed my best friend!"

"Oh, no, I'm not—" And then I stop myself. I need help, right? Would it be totally wrong for me to let her think I'm this Rebecca girl? Just for an hour or so. What's the harm?

"I'm happy to be here," I finish. Guilt fills me, but I have no choice. If someone doesn't help me soon, I'm going to be spending the night in the woods, alone and scared.

"Come in from the cold! Oh, I'm so pleased that you've arrived! My visit at Harksbury has been quite dull, you see. I've been here just three weeks and am weary of the monotony. Where are your things?" She talks with her hands a lot, throwing them all over in her enthusiasm.

"Huh?" I see that she's looking behind me, and I turn around to see an empty stoop. Oh, right. If I had come straight from America, I'd have luggage. "They, er, washed overboard in a storm. I lost everything."

"Such a pity! Well, no matter, we appear to be the same size. Are you wearing men's clothing? How embarrassed you must be!"

I blush, even though I'm not sure why. She's wearing a lavender dress with ruffles, and *I'm* the one who should be embarrassed? Who is this girl? And why is she dressed like that? British people are really odd. I bet this is one of those really formal, old-fashioned families. Maybe aristocrats or something.

"Can I use your telephone?" I blurt out. If I can get a hold of Mrs. Bentley, all this will be over soon. I'll be back in my room, taking a shower and putting on my warm fuzzy slippers.

The girl stops and tips her head to the side as she looks at me, like a dog would when it is trying to hear you better. Her brown curls bounce around like a shampoo commercial. "A what?"

"Telephone." I try to keep my voice from sounding as desperate as I feel.

She scrunches her cute little nose. "I don't think so."

Tears spring to my eyes, but I blink them back. She probably has some fancy iPhone she doesn't want me to use. She probably thinks I'd steal it.

"How about, uh, a ride into town?" I say. "For, uh, clothes. Since I lost all mine." The lump in my throat grows until the last few words come out as a mere squeak.

"Town? At this hour? We'll go together first thing in the morning. I've a mind to buy some new ribbon. Until then you shall rest! His Grace has already retired for the evening, and I was only just on my way to my quarters myself, when I heard your voice. Let us get you settled and we shall go to town together in the morn."

"But—it's important. Please. It will be a quick trip." I hate myself, but my lip actually trembles like a little kid, until I bite it so hard I can taste blood.

The girl looks confused. She stares at me with a furrowed brow, and I don't like it; I get the feeling she knows something's up, that I'm not really Rebecca. If she realizes I'm a fraud, I'll be back on the road, walking—and trying to figure out what this girl, and her weird act, is all about. "I couldn't possibly send for the carriage at this hour without His Grace's permission. He may be my cousin, but I wouldn't dare wake him. You'll have to wait for the morn."

I don't even care that she said carriage and not car. I swallow, biting back the urge to beg and plead, and instead nod. I'm going to miss the whole thing tonight. I was really going to get the guts to go to that club.

What's worse is I know by the time I get back to the hotel tomorrow, Mrs. Bentley will probably have an entire search and rescue team looking for me, but it's not like I have other options.

"Okay, it can wait until tomorrow," I say. "I'm, uh, happy to be here."

She smiles and grabs my hand and drags me into the entry, and all I can think is *ow, ow, ow* with each step, until I'm inside and my mind goes completely blank, I'm so mesmerized. The foyer is huge, with thirty-foot arched ceilings and a grand staircase so big it could fit a hundred people. On the wall behind the steps is a mural at least twenty feet across, some kind of woodsy scene with leaping horses. The steps split on a landing halfway up, and then turn in opposite directions, toward separate wings.

This place is like a museum. Except bigger and fancier. The expansive floor is marble or granite or something, with an inlaid pattern that leads in all different directions, down long hallways and up to impressive oak doors. There's elegant oak molding and carved wood details all over the walls and ceilings, and huge portraits in gold frames hanging so far up the walls it would take a twenty-foot ladder to hang them. The toe of my Prada heel is resting on a colorful patterned rug, complete with tassels at two ends.

These people have money. With a capital M. More than necessary. I bet they have a private jet somewhere out back and their own airstrip.

"Come. Follow me."

I half expect her voice to echo in the cavernous space, but it doesn't. I follow her toward the stairs, but as I climb the first step, my heel catches and I go down, landing hard on my knees.

That's all it takes. I burst into tears in a heap on the second step. This is too much. I don't understand any of this and I don't want to. I just want it to be over. I want to be home and comfortable and happy, and I'm so far away I don't even know where I am. Why did this happen to me? What did I do to deserve this?

I was miserable this morning, and it's even worse now. What else could go wrong?

"Rebecca?" The girl scuffles back down the steps and when she touches my shoulder, I flinch away.

I don't know how long it takes for me to compose myself, reeling back in the tears and wiping my nose on the shoulder of my T-shirt, but when I look up she's still standing there. "I'm, um, I'm sorry. It's just been a long . . . journey."

She nods as if she understands, and I run my fingers under my eyes and try to sniffle away the snot that is probably hanging out of my nose.

I don't say anything as I follow her up the rest of the stairs. Emily shows me down a hall that stretches on forever, door after door, until I can't even see the front entry at all anymore. The house is dark and eerie, candlelight flickering as we pass, making our shadows dance.

She opens a door for me and points inside, mumbles something about a maid, then leaves.

I walk in, shove the door shut behind me, and walk over to my bed. I throw myself down on top of the covers, bury my face in a lumpy pillow, and cry.

5

There's someone in my room. I know it before I see her, because she's making a grunting noise, and there's some kind of scraping sound. I spring upright in bed, the blanket pulled up to my chin.

And that's when I remember. Last night . . . walking through the woods . . . all these people pretending they live in the past. My chest gets hollow and achy, I'm so homesick. I bite down on my lip, hard, to keep the tears at bay.

I was supposed to wake up at the hotel. I was supposed to laugh at that funny dream I had. Or even wake up in the hospital after hitting my head so hard. It wasn't supposed to be real.

I wasn't supposed to wake up here.

But I did. I'm in the same bedroom. It's bigger than my living room back home, with a four-poster bed that probably wouldn't even *fit* in my own bedroom. The walls are painted a sunny yellow, which I hadn't noticed last night in the dim light of the candles. There's a fire in my room; when was that

PRADA & PREJUDICE

lit? Its flames are dancing below an ornate mantle painted in white with gold accents.

These people are really into their gold accents. There are carvings around every door and window, painted to match the mantle. There's not a single plain surface anywhere— every golden-yellow wall has paintings or elaborate molding or decorative tapestries covering half of it. Even the curtains, which are slung carelessly open, are a rich and vibrant gold. The ceilings are high, probably fifteen feet or higher.

I don't know what this place is, but it's huge and fancy and *expensive.* It's like a bed-and-breakfast for rich aristocrats or something.

It's a servant who woke me up. I can tell by the look of her. She is in a plain black dress, with her mousy hair pulled back in a low bun. She's pretty, even without any makeup, with a fresh face that belongs in a Noxzema commercial. When she smiles at me, it somehow quells the panic that is steadily rising in my stomach.

The girl is dragging a trunk. She stops by the big armoire and flings it open. "I've four dresses fer ye te choose from," she says. She has a funny accent. It's British, but it's not all prim and proper-sounding like Emily's. "We must hurry or ye'll be late. The duke'll be joining the ladies fer breakfast on yer account."

I shoot out of bed like a rocket, the panic back in full force. "*Duke?* What does that mean?"

She looks at me like I've grown a second head. "'m sorry?"

"*Who* is a duke?"

30

"His Grace, o'course."

I just stare at her, my heart quickening to a thunderous roar. "A guy named Grace is a duke?"

She snorts, and then covers her mouth like the reaction was inappropriate. "'Is name is not Grace. 'E's Lord Alexander Thorton-Hawke. The Duke of Harksbury."

"So why did you just call him Grace?"

She lifts an eyebrow at me. "I forget ye'r American. The appropriate way te address 'im—and any other duke—is *Your Grace*."

"Oh."

I sit down on the edge of the bed. My legs are too shaky to hold me up. So I've landed myself in the house of a duke.

Now I get why the house is so fancy. But what does that mean? Is he royalty? He's probably going to hate me.

Oh God. What if he knows Rebecca (aka, the girl I am *not*) better than Emily? What if he knows I'm not her? Dukes have power, right? What if he has me arrested or throws me in a dungeon or something? This place is huge. Like a castle. They probably *have* a dungeon. No one will ever find me. Not in a foreign country in the middle of nowhere.

I start breathing heavily, my breath coming out in rasps. I need air.

"Are ye okay?"

I don't move or nod or even acknowledge her. I just keep staring at the edge of the rug beneath my toes.

God, why did I ever say I was Rebecca? This is never going to work. I should have told Emily the truth. Maybe she would have helped me even if I was a stranger. She seemed nice. I could have just asked for help instead of pretending to be someone else.

Even if she hadn't helped I could have kept walking. Maybe town isn't really that far. I could be there now, instead of in the house of a duke who will probably have me beheaded or something.

Ten minutes pass, my breathing returns to normal, and I feel a little better. I just have to get through breakfast. If the duke doesn't realize I'm not Rebecca in the first second I meet him, I can probably pull it off. I'll just stare down at my plate and stay quiet. Then Emily will take me to town and I'll bail and run for it. She won't know what hit her.

The servant just kind of stands there and waits for me, without saying anything. She doesn't even act like she thinks I'm crazy, thank God. I don't think I could take that on top of everything else. Finally, I pull myself together and stand up.

The girl picks up some clothing and throws it over the edge of the bed. I'm so not a dress person, but I have way bigger things to worry about.

I take a deep, soothing breath, focusing on the things in front of me.

Once I get to town I don't have to play their games—I'll hail a taxi and get back to the hotel. Mrs. Bentley will yell at me for freaking her out, we'll all have a good laugh, and then I'll continue on my trip. My mom will probably ground me when I get back home, but at this point *home* sounds so heavenly I could care less.

God, what if the shoes have something to do with it? This

all happened the second I put them on. Maybe they're cursed or something.

"Breakfast's served in twenty minutes. We best hurry."

At the mention of food, my stomach growls so loudly it sounds like a wounded cat. The maid pretends not to notice. Before I can figure out what the girl is doing, she's pulling my T-shirt off over my head and I'm naked. Guess she's not worried about my modesty.

I stand with one arm crossed over my chest until she forces my arms above my head so she can slip on a thin scratchy gown, and then she's yanking my jeans off and throwing other things over my head and lacing them up.

I swear she puts six layers on me, though it's probably more like three. The dress is a pretty peach color, with white trim on the bottom and the neckline. She ties a little white sash just under my bust, making an empire waist.

It's cute, actually. I'd never wear it at home of course, but here, it kind of works.

Now that I'm wearing it, though, I'm filled with the overwhelming desire to yank it back off. I can't wear this. I can't be like them and pretend this is ancient history and that wearing stuff like this is normal.

I start to walk away. I need my jeans. I need . . . normalcy.

But the maid takes me by the shoulders, shuffles me over to a stool, and forcibly plops me down on it. Next thing I know, she's brushing my hair. *Hard.* I swear she must rip out thirty strands with the first swipe, because my scalp is screaming.

I grimace my way through her hair styling, and within ten

minutes she's done. I reach my hand up and feel gently around the top of my head. She's turned my hair into some kind of braided updo, twisted around my head like a crown.

She hands me a pair of gloves, and I plan to just hold onto them, but then I realize she expects me to wear them now. Indoors. It seems sort of silly but I slip them on anyway.

I try on the slippers she's brought me, but they're way too small. Emily and I might share a dress size, but we definitely differ when it comes to feet. The maid finds my Prada heels, and even though my toes still hurt and I've officially decided that the heels are the bane of my existence, I slip them on. It's not like I can go barefoot.

By the time I'm limping down the stairs, my dress trailing behind me on the steps, I don't even feel like I'm myself anymore. From my braided hair to this ancient-style dress, I'm someone else. I've stepped into a dream.

Or maybe a nightmare.

A servant shows me down a hall, and it seems to extend forever and ever. The house is huge, a labyrinth of doors and halls that extend further than I can see. It reminds me of my high school. Except fancier.

The halls are tall and wide, yet still a little dark. There aren't any light fixtures. Or light switches. Instead there are paintings everywhere, and patterned carpeting, and thick carved casings around each door. Many of the windows have deep bays with seats, and others are made of leaded glass, some colored. It feels a little eerie to walk down the hall, dressed like this, like I'm part of it all.

I stop, close my eyes, and breathe in and out slowly, concentrating on the sound, trying to ignore the feeling of the dress brushing against my legs. This isn't real.

I open my eyes, but I'm still standing here.

God, I need to get away.

When I walk into the dining room, Emily is inside, and my eyes dart to meet those of the two strangers: an overweight woman in her late forties who looks like she's wearing a giant doily and a guy who looks much closer to my age. That's the duke? He's probably nineteen! Before I can get a better look at him, the woman barrels at me, her arms outstretched.

"Miss Rebecca," she says, and then wraps me in a bear hug. "It's so wonderful to see you! Your journey must have been a hasty one, you're so early! I must apologize for not greeting you last night."

I can't breathe. All I can smell is an overpowering powdery scent coming from this lady. *People in the olden days really liked their powders, huh?*

I'm so shocked by my own thoughts that I jerk upright, out of her grasp. Why had I thought something like that? This isn't the olden days. It's just some people who choose not to live in today's world. But it's still the twenty-first century. There's no way I'm actually *back in time*. No way.

I force myself to turn away from the woman and look at the guy standing next to her. And when I do, I lose my breath entirely.

The duke.

6

This guy is a *duke*. How can he be a duke when he's only a few years older than me?

He's dressed in an old-fashioned way, like the others, but somehow on him . . . it's different. His navy jacket accentuates his broad shoulders and narrow waist. Snug buckskin pants cover his long, lean legs, and his knee-high leather boots make it all . . . fancy? And yet even in the ridiculous getup, he looks formal and intimidating, and somehow kind of hot too. How can a guy dressed like that look so *good?*

He walks toward me, and I almost step backward, but manage to keep my heels glued to the floor. He has dark hair, and up close I see that his eyes are a vibrant shade of green. They almost glow. And he's tall. Even from a few feet away, I know he'll tower over me.

He's staring. I swallow as I stare back, waiting for it. Waiting for the moment his eyes shift, waiting for the moment when he realizes I'm a fraud. My heart pounds as he stares at me, his face completely blank. What is he thinking? Does he know? God, what if he really does have some creepy dungeon?

"Miss Rebecca," he says, bowing toward me.

And so I curtsy. I actually curtsy like it's the natural thing to do. I don't even know how to, but I cross one foot behind the other and lower myself toward the ground. It's not exactly effortless, but I don't trip over my feet or the hem of the skirt so I consider it an accomplishment.

"I trust you had a safe journey?" His voice is beautiful— deep and a little rough, like a guy's voice should be, with that same aristocratic English accent.

"Yes, er, thanks." I smile shakily at him, but he just nods and returns to his seat. Obviously, he is not a people person.

I walk over to the table and take a seat across from Emily. I notice she has a pair of gloves sitting beside her, so I slip mine off and set them on the table as she has done.

There are three servants in the room; they stand silently against the walls, peculiarly identical to one another in height, like they came in a matching set.

The duke raises his arm and sort of flicks his wrist, and they swoop into action, coming at me with a platter full of food. The first guy is holding a tower of eggs.

Ew. I don't do eggs. "Oh, um, no thank you, I'm not an egg person."

All noise stops. Everyone stares at me.

Am I not supposed to talk to the servants?

I smile weakly at the duke and his mother as the servant walks away, and another approaches with ham.

I clamp my mouth shut as he plops a hearty portion down on my plate.

My mouth is suddenly very dry. I turn to the servant standing motionless behind me. "Can I get some water?"

Yeah. Definitely not supposed to talk to them. The guy's eyes flicker over to the old lady, as if he needs permission to get me some water.

"There is lemonade in front of you," the old lady says.

"Oh." Is that what that is?

I take a quick swallow and try not to choke. This obviously is not Country Time, if you know what I mean.

I was starving ten minutes ago, but now that I'm sitting in the same room as these weird people, my appetite is gone. This breakfast needs to be over, stat. I can barely keep up with the glove and servant etiquette; I'm bound to screw something up. I need to maintain my fake identity, wrangle a ride to town, and say *sayonara*.

Alex's (am I allowed to call him that?) chair is bigger than he is, which is an accomplishment given his size. The back of it has all these scrolling details along the top, and it dwarfs his broad shoulders. It's like a throne, really. Maybe dukes *are* royals.

"I was quite surprised when Emily told me you were wearing *trousers* when you arrived," the old woman says. She's cutting into her ham, her hands delicately gripping the silverware. "How terribly embarrassing."

Wow. Rude, much? Why does she have to talk to me at all? Let's just shovel a bunch of breakfast in our mouths and get out of here. I need to leave *now*.

But she's staring at me, waiting for a response. She's sitting back in her chair, carefully bringing tiny bites of food to her mouth without leaning forward the slightest bit.

Well, I might as well stick with my story. "Yes, um, my nicer things were lost. I had no other choice."

The lady takes a bite of food, and for one blissful second I think she's going to leave me alone. But alas, I am not that lucky. "I trust your father has seen to it that your studies are not neglected?"

Another tiny bite. This lady eats like a bird. In comparison, I feel like a caveman with a drumstick.

I nod my head, trying to think of something safe to say. "Yes, of course. I'm particularly talented in science and math."

Her mouth curls up in disdain. "Such . . . masculine topics! Has he not taught you the arts? French? Music?"

Masculine? God, who does this lady think she is? She's lucky I *have* to be nice to her. "Oh, uh, yes. I also love literature and poetry," I say.

To be honest, I don't really like either. Science and math . . . Those are so simple and straightforward. Poetry? It's so up in the air and hard to interpret. I never get what the poet is trying to say. Katie did half my English homework freshman year just to ensure I didn't fail.

"Well, thank goodness for that. Your mother was the granddaughter of a marquess, you know. You may not be titled, but at least you can cling to that, can't you?"

Huh? Is she serious? I'm supposed to cling to some distant relation in an effort to feel good enough? I don't even know how to begin to tell her what is wrong with that.

And then she speaks. *Again.* I grind my teeth together and take another deep breath. "Emily tells me you plan to visit town this morn?"

I nod and shove another bite of salty ham in my mouth. If this lady keeps up the twenty questions, who knows what I'm going to blurt out?

The old woman gives me a tight smile. "I'd love to join you,"—*Oh dang*—"But I've some letters to attend to. Perhaps another time."

I nod and try to feign some kind of disappointment, but I'm sure it doesn't look real. She's annoying me already, the way she has a little upturned nose and beauty queen posture, like she's better than everyone else at the table.

I do my best to ignore her completely and act as if a painting of a pond and geese is the most interesting thing I've ever seen. It's hanging over another fancy carved hearth, this one glowing with hot coals. Despite the fact that it's summer, this place feels cold, even with the morning sun streaming through big arched windows. There are pillars on each side of the fire, carved busts perched precariously on top.

I wonder if they're actually marble sculptures of the duke himself. I can't tell from this angle. Either way, the idea is amusing. I can totally see a guy like him wanting a stone carved bust of himself. He's probably pretty narcissistic, given that he's not socializing with anyone else at the table. His intense green eyes are too busy concentrating on his breakfast plate to notice anyone.

Emily finally speaks. She's been nearly silent, unlike the bubbly personality she'd had last night. I wonder if it has anything to do with this annoying old lady. Emily smiles at her, but it doesn't reach her hazel eyes. "Do you intend to join us at the country-dance on the morrow, Your Grace?"

Country-dance? Somehow I can't picture the old lady dancing.

The lady—also known as Grace, for some reason—shakes her head so vigorously her gray curls bounce. "I do not intend to . . . I believe I shall get some rest instead. I feel I'm coming down with something. Perhaps Rebecca could join you?" She turns to look at me. "We'd not expected your arrival so soon, but I am sure your company would be most welcome at the Pommeroy Estate."

I just smile and nod. I'll be long gone before any country-dance takes place, but I don't say that. The mere *idea* of joining these people at a country-dance is laugh-out-loud funny.

Silence settles over the table for all of two-point-five seconds before the lady looks at me again. "And where is your father? I cannot believe he would allow you to travel such a distance unchaperoned!"

I stare at her. She's not suspicious of me, is she? What if all these questions are really her attempt to catch me in a lie? "Oh, no, he's pretty trusting," I say.

Can't Emily jump in here? She's just sitting there, perfectly erect in a sea-green gown, silently chewing on a biscuit.

Victoria thins her lips, and it accentuates all the fine lines in her face. She's got to be pushing fifty years old. "Even so, he's obviously remiss in his duties. You should have been raised in a proper household. Tell me, has he looked after your marriage prospects? Your mother was such a dear friend of mine, but even so, I worry that he's done you a disservice by not remarrying."

I choke on the biscuit I'm eating. She's calling herself a dear friend of my supposedly deceased mother in one breath, and then in the next, wishing my father had remarried? I do *not* like this lady. "I . . . uh . . ." I swallow slowly. "I don't want to get married until I'm thirty."

"Thirty!" she says. "That is ridiculous! This can not be what it has come to in America. How do you expect to cope until then? I think I must write to your father immediately, for he seems to be allowing you too many liberties!"

Is she for real? Like she can just write a note to my dad and he's going to send me off to the chapel, or what? If she knew how little my dad actually cared about me, she wouldn't be saying that! "I'll be fine on my own. It's not like I *need* a guy or something."

This feels a little bit like defending my no-boyfriend status to myself. This is the part where I assure myself that it's okay that guys don't really pay attention to me. This is the part where I say I don't actually want or need a boyfriend, and then smile into the mirror as if I believe it. Really though, I'm ready for somebody to sweep me off my feet like all those silly movies I watch with only a bowl of popcorn for company.

But Victoria doesn't need to know it. She just looks taken aback for a moment, like what I'd said was beyond rude or something. I bite down, hard, on my lip. I need to shut up, or this is going to turn into Trisha Marks: Part 2. I'll blurt out something stupid and get myself into yet another mess. Why am I arguing? Why am I allowing her to bait me?

"But how can you possibly expect to live? I should think that would be quite a difficult life. You can not be capable of managing on your own."

I try to stop myself, but it doesn't work. The words come flooding out. "It's not difficult at all. In fact, if marriage is anything like *you* seem to think it is, I want nothing to do with it. I'll be happy if I remain single forever! So you can forget about planning my wedding, I don't want it!" I push my plate away so fast half the contents spill onto the white linens.

This whole surreal, crappy day is catching up to me and everything is spiraling out of control.

"You will bite your tongue!"

That's it. I shove back from the table and my chair topples over and nearly knocks into the servant who had stepped forward to grab it. Everything is crashing down around me, and I can't handle any of this anymore. "I will not! I don't know who you think you are, or what in God's name you guys think you're doing acting like this, but you don't have the right to rule *my life*." Before I know what I'm doing I spin around, my skirts twirling, and rush toward the door. When I get there I look back at the table. "You guys are all *crazy*."

And then I turn and run. I can't even feel the pain or blisters on my feet anymore as my sight blurs with tears.

What the heck am I doing? I know I just made things so

much worse. I know I need them to help me. But it's too late to stop now.

Down the hall, I find the foyer, where a man opens the door for me, and I burst outside as if reality will find me on the other side and I can leave all this craziness behind.

It's not there, of course. It's just more of the expansive lawn and the long drive. I'm still standing here in this ridiculous dress.

The door clicks open and I turn around, praying it's Emily, but it's not.

It's the duke. The second I see the toe of his leather boots, my heart leaps into my throat. My eyes travel up his long legs and over his waist and chest, until I get to his face, and my heart sinks. He's ticked. He's across the stoop in a half second, his strides so long and purposeful I have to fight the urge to just *run*.

"Might I remind you that you are a guest in my home?" His words come out so loud and harsh it's impossible not to wince.

I open my mouth to say something but I have no idea how I'm supposed to respond. It doesn't look like he wanted an answer anyway, because he just surges ahead. "You may be from America but you are in England, and you'll do well to adhere to the rules of society. You will *not* insult the dowager again."

"Then tell her to leave me *alone!*"

He takes one more step, so he's inches away. "It may be acceptable to speak as you do where you come from. But in my world, we respect our elders and our superiors."

"She's not my superior. And neither are you."

"I outrank you," he says, half spitting the words as he edges even closer.

"So? Does that make you better than me?" I put one hand on my hip and clench the other in a fist.

"Yes, it does!" he thunders.

"Ugh! You're unbelievable," I say. "I've never met anyone so arrogant in my life."

"No? Well, I've never met anyone so insolent! You are certainly not the prim little *Rebecca* my mother was expecting."

My lips part slightly and I stare back at him, my anger twisting with fear. Why did he emphasize *Rebecca*? What is he saying? Does he know I'm not her?

I grasp at the fury I'd felt just moments ago, but it's slipping away.

He doesn't explain, just spins around and stalks away. I'm left staring at the door as it slams shut behind him.

7

I'm halfway down the stairs when the sounds of a carriage echo, and I stop, one foot on the cobbled drive and one on the stone steps. When I glance upward, I see Emily walk out the door, a mischievous grin on her cherub face. "I've never seen Her Grace look so shocked in all her life!" she giggles, and despite everything, I smile at her. I can't believe I'm actually smiling after all this.

I kind of want to take her with me when I go. She doesn't deserve to live here with these people. They're all mean and crazy, and she's just nice.

I try to shrug away the worry that the duke is setting up his dungeon as we speak and instead turn toward the carriage rolling up, two shiny black horses pulling it. I just stand there and stare for what seems like eternity, wondering if I should really get inside that thing. And then I pinch myself. For real, I reach over and pinch my arm, leaving a nasty red mark behind, but I'm still standing here. Yesterday, I was sitting in a twenty-

first-century café in London, bemoaning my lack of friends . . .
and now look at me: braided hair, old-fashioned dress, and I'm
about to get into a carriage. A real-life, horse-drawn carriage.

"So, uh, how far is town?" I ask Emily as a servant helps
me into the carriage.

"Twelve miles," Emily says. She's sitting on a bench atop
the carriage, arranging her skirts.

My heart jumps into my throat.

If we're really twelve miles away, how did I get this far?
The carriage takes a left out of Harksbury, so I mentally add
a few more miles from where I'd woken up. Fifteen miles?
Who would drive an unconscious person fifteen miles into
the woods and drop her off? And even if someone did, is
fifteen miles far enough from London for the scenery to look
this . . . rustic?

My only warped explanation is melting away, and as I
watch the scenery roll by, a new explanation is nibbling at the
edges of my mind.

The carriage rides roughly, every bump jarring me nearly out
of the seat. There are curtains pulled open and tied to the side,
so we'll have enough light to see by. I can't believe how noisy
and drafty the whole thing is. We pass a couple carriages, and
there are servants dressed just like the ones driving us. Emily
is chatting away about the royal family, something about a ball
or a mask or something, and then I get an idea.

"Wait, um, I forget . . . Who is the king these days?"

She laughs and playfully smacks my arm. "America is so
isolated, isn't it? An entire continent away! The king is not

truly our ruler, of course. Our monarch is the prince regent."

I nod and swallow the lump in my throat. Last year I had to take world history, including several chapters on the royal families of a dozen different countries. A prince regent . . . England hasn't had one of those since the early 1800s.

Okay, so they're really committed to their entire act. They probably have textbooks they refer to every night to make sure they get the details right.

It's a feeble excuse and it doesn't make sense anymore. Not when I watch as home after home rolls past, each of them looking older than the last. Not when the roads are so clearly prehistoric, with ruts and mud puddles.

Not when I haven't seen a single piece of ordinary trash, or a lamppost, or a broken-down car. A chill races down my spine. This isn't right. Everything is just . . . all off and unfamiliar.

I'm sitting in a carriage, for god's sake.

Emily must sense I don't want to talk to her because she leaves me alone as I stare at everything trailing by. It seems to be going faster and faster as the heavy feeling in my stomach grows to the size of a bowling ball.

Even if we *were* just playing make-believe, there would be something, right? Some clue, some overlap of the real world. But if I admit that maybe I'm not with crazy people, that maybe this *isn't* fake, what does that mean?

Around an hour later, as we get closer to town, the buildings become steadily closer together, until the carriage rolls to a stop near the sidewalk and I jump out so fast the servant who'd planned to help me nearly falls to the ground.

"Sorry!" I say, and then I scurry over to the shop nearest me and press my nose to the glass. There has to be something: a magazine, an orange extension cord, a Starbucks cup.

But there's nothing. I sprint down the block and look into the next store. I can feel Emily staring after me, her feet rooted to the place I left her.

This entire town . . . this village . . . there's nothing out of place. And it's *not* London at all. I'm far, far away from the hotel, and anything else I know.

I trudge back to Emily, my feet scraping along like fifty-pound weights. I feel as if I've just gone ten rounds in a boxing ring only to emerge defeated.

Emily is twisting a pretty ruffled parasol around in circles and staring at me with her best WTF look.

"Um, so, I have a question," I say. She already thinks I'm crazy.

And she's about to think I'm crazier.

"Yes?" Emily says.

"What year is it?"

She laughs. "Though I am sure your journey felt torturously long, it's but a month since your last letter. It is yet 1815."

1815. Right.

"I mean, not here," I say, motioning in our general vicinity. "I mean in the real world. In the *whole* world, and not just your world." I wave my hands around for emphasis.

"I'm afraid I don't understand your meaning," she says.

And then I slump to the ground. Town was supposed to be my saving grace. I was supposed to find a telephone, or a taxi, or something that would make sense. Because since the moment I tripped in these stupid heels, nothing has.

I pull my legs up around me and bury my face in my knees. The skirts of this peach dress are scratchy on my face, but I don't care. The fabric dampens with my tears.

Emily stands next to me. I can just make out the hem of her skirt in my glittering vision. "Rebecca?" she says, her voice concerned. She's shifting back and forth on her feet; I can see her dress sway with the movement.

I want to yell at her, *"Callie! My name is Callie!"* But I can't. What if I'm really stuck here? What if I have to be Rebecca forever? Of course, that won't work. The real Rebecca will arrive. In a month, according to Emily. And then what?

God, when did everything turn upside down? I go on a summer trip abroad, and then I start running two hundred years behind schedule?

Somehow I doubt that's quite what they had in mind when they said we'd be studying European History.

How does something like this even happen? It's not like I jumped in a black hole or tried to invent a time machine or . . . anything. Just *BAM*, and I'm here. My throat aches and my arms and legs are now a thousand pounds. I don't want to move. Ever.

"Er, Rebecca?" she says again.

I don't want to be Rebecca. I want to curl in a ball and close my eyes, and I want to see cars and smog when I open them up again.

But if I keep acting like this, Emily's going to be watching me. Closely. And I can't let her do that, because she'll start to think dear old Rebecca belongs in the loony bin. I've heard way too many horror stories about old asylums to allow that to happen. So she can't know I'm really Callie Montgomery, twenty-first-century high school girl. Telling everyone I'm a time-traveling freak will only make things worse.

"Uh, yeah, sorry," I say, my voice hoarse. "I'm just worn out, I think. I guess town . . . uh . . . changed more than I remember." I climb to my feet and try to wipe all the dirt from my skirts.

"Oh! I'd not thought of that. Yes, it's certainly grown, hasn't it? My home is nearly a full day's ride from here, and I'm afraid I don't visit as often as I'd like. I was quite impressed by the growth in the last few years." There's a note of pride in her voice, like she wants to brag about how large the town is when I'm pretty sure I can see all the way to the end of it from where I stand.

I nod but I don't speak again because I can't swallow the lump in my throat.

I want my mom, to be honest. Even though just thinking that makes me feel like I'm five instead of fifteen.

Emily turns and heads back to the carriage, but I just stand there, firmly rooted to the sidewalk. We can't just go back. Not yet. I'm not done here. There has to be something or someone who can help me.

I take one step and my heel catches on a cobble. I barely manage to stop myself before I face plant.

Oh God. These shoes! What if it's the shoes? That's exactly

what happened before. Maybe I could buy a new pair of shoes and wear them, and maybe that would fix everything.

I turn around and look up and down the walk. It's not like I'll find a Prada shop. But they obviously make shoes somewhere, right?

I stalk past several stores, peering in the windows. Someone makes shoes. They have to.

"Rebecca?" Emily's voice calls after me as I pass another shop. The shoes will fix everything. I'll put on some of those weird slipper-style things and once I walk out of the shop, I'll be back in London. The Prada heels are just cursed or something.

I pass another store. This one has little teacups in the window.

This is ridiculous. Don't girls like shoes here?

Oh. Wait. Even if I find a shoe store, how am I supposed to pay for the shoes?

Maybe I don't need the shoes, per se. Maybe I just need to take these stupid ones off. I unbuckle the straps over my foot, pick up the heel, and fling one shoe down the walkway.

Liberated, I pull the other heel off and fling it down with its mate.

Now what?

Should I fall over? On purpose?

That's how it worked before. I had to knock my head on the sidewalk. I eye the big cobbles beneath my bare toes. They look so *hard*.

What if I have a real concussion? Last year, Mike Lange,

star quarterback, had to sit out two games because he had a concussion. We lost both games because of it, but supposedly if he got another one within a couple weeks of the first, his brain could swell and he'd get brain damage.

Which doesn't really sound that fun.

Emily clears her throat.

I chew on my lip and look down the walkway at my shoes. What am I, crazy? I just flung four-hundred-dollar pumps down the street.

"Shall we shall return to Harksbury? Your journey must have tired you more than you expected. You need proper rest, yes?"

She's looking at me like I've gone a little loco, her cute button nose wrinkled up and her wide hazel eyes narrowed to tiny little slits.

How am I going to return to Harksbury after telling them all off? Maybe knocking my head wouldn't be *that* bad.

Stay calm. That's what everyone says about emergencies. You have to stay calm and everything will resolve itself.

"Yes. Let me, uh, let me go grab my shoes." I hobble, barefoot, down the walk and retrieve my pumps, jam my feet back into them, and then follow her back to the carriage. The servants are silent, but I know they're staring at me when my back is turned. I have to pull it together. I can't just lose it like that, throwing my shoes like I'm in a shot-put competition.

If I think clearly, maybe I'll come up with a real plan.

But until then, my name is Rebecca. I am a prim and proper Regency girl. I wear dresses and I curtsy.

I belong here.

8

I've been sitting in a window seat in my bedroom for twenty minutes, my forehead pressed against the cool glass window, when I see Alex. He's standing in what I guess is the backyard, facing the stables and talking to a servant. How many servants are there? These people must be really, truly rich. I've already seen close to twenty so far, between the gardeners, the maids, the butler, the grooms . . . and I'm assuming they have a cook or two.

I study him, knowing he has no clue he's being watched. His hair is a little longer than I realized, sort of an Orlando in *Pirates of the Caribbean* kind of look. His jacket has actual coattails, which I hadn't noticed this morning, and even from here, I can tell it's well fitted.

Even though he's pretty hot, he also kinda looks like he's one of the Village People. I snicker to myself and that's when he turns around and looks up. There's no way he could have heard me, but I feel as if I've been caught red-handed, and I recoil so quickly I fall backward off the window seat. There's a rug on the ground next to the seat, but even so, I land with a hard thud that knocks the wind out of me. Even though I'm trying hard to be Rebecca, I just pulled another Callie classic. For a long moment I just lie there, staring at the ceiling, catching my breath and wondering if he knew I was watching him. He knows which room I'm in, right? Even if he hadn't seen my face, he'd know it was me. My skirts are fanned out around me, and I twist them in my fingers while I try to decide if I should be embarrassed.

I crawl back toward the seat and peek out over it, but I realize with some degree of disappointment he's gone. The expansive lawn is empty. Is it pathetic if I wanted to check him out some more? He might be a jerk, but at least he's good eye-candy.

I get up and walk back over to my bed, plopping down on it with a heavy sigh.

I'm smart, right? I should be able to come up with a solid plan as to how I can get back to the twenty-first century.

The trouble is I'm lost without Wikipedia and Google. I know all sorts of things, of course, but none of it is useful: the periodic table of elements, how to factor a math equation with four different variables, the symbiotic relationship between the great white shark and the remora fish. Completely useless, random information.

Even a year of advanced chemistry isn't going to do me any good; it's not like there's a chapter in there about time travel.

I get up off the bed and creep to the door and peek out. No one is around.

I'll just explore the house. Maybe there really is a phone hidden somewhere that will prove Emily is lying about 1815. Or maybe I'll find a servant in some Old Navy jeans.

My room is on the second floor of the west wing, at the end of the hall, so all I can do is go toward the front entry. There are doors on both sides of the hall, so I walk toward the first one and press my ear to it. Silence.

I ease the doorknob around and push it inward, cringing as the hinges creak. It's just another bedroom, slightly smaller than mine. This one has hideous red wallpaper with flowers swirling up and down in vertical stripes, and carpet in the exact same shade of crimson.

Ugh. This is definitely not going to help me.

I exit the room and continue down the hall. I poke my head in a couple of rooms and see more beds. How many bedrooms does one house need? I haven't even seen Emily, Victoria, or Alex's rooms. That makes at least seven or eight bedrooms . . . and that's without seeing the other 90 percent of this place.

I get that he's a duke, but isn't this kind of overkill?

I skip the next couple of doors, figuring they're all bedrooms. Toward the front of the hall is a set of double doors, which must mean the room is something different. I see a servant walking up the stairs, so I act like I'm just casually fixing my hair until she disappears into a bedroom.

I ease open one of the two doors and poke my head in.

A *library*. I can't help the grin that spreads across my face. There's got to be something here I can use. Maybe there will be modern books. Or even just old ones that might hold some useful information I could glean from their pages.

I inhale the scent of paper and books as I shut the door behind me and step inside. There are dozens of shelves—rows and rows of them. They tower over my head. There's even one of those old ladders attached to the wall.

I run my fingers over the spines and walk down the rows, looking at the titles. *Utopia. The Miser. Robinson Crusoe.* Katie would go all geeky if she were here with me right now . . . She loves literature, especially anything in first edition. She collects books like she collects MySpace friends.

The books are all leather, and the titles are old. I pause at a collection of Shakespeare. *Othello. Romeo and Juliet. A Midsummer Night's Dream.* I pull *Hamlet* out and look at it, but then set it back down on the shelf.

I pass a row of books on philosophy, and another on astrology. Up and down I go, pausing now and then, but not pulling any books out. I'm not sure what I expected to find. *The Idiot's Guide to Time Travel*?

Whatever it is, it's not here.

I round the last shelf and go over to the sofa and plop down on it. This is all so . . . tiring. I want to be home. In my bed. I want to wake up and watch Saturday morning cartoons with a bowl of cereal. I lie back on a pillow, my dress draped over my legs and hanging over the edge of the cushions, toward the floor.

Oh, what am I doing? Hanging out in this library isn't going to do me any good. I've got to keep searching.

I sit up and stare down at my shoes. Maybe if I were wearing something more comfortable, walking around the house wouldn't suck so much. I reach down to adjust the buckle, loosening it one notch. As I go to adjust the other shoe, I see something. It's a stack of papers, shoved between the small table and the leg of the couch. I reach down and slide them out. There's a ribbon around them, so that the bundle is a few inches thick. They're letters. The wax seals are broken, so it's clear they've been read. I slip the ribbon off.

That's when I hear the door click open. What do I do? Hide? Oh God, I'm probably not supposed to be digging around in here, picking up letters that are not mine. And what if this room is supposed to be off-limits?

Panicked, I duck behind the sofa, the stack of papers still in my hand. It's elevated off the floor with four spindly legs, so I can make out the shoes of the person stepping inside.

I recognize the leather riding boots of Alex. The duke.

Crap. Why am I hiding? Doesn't this look suspicious? The letters practically burn in my hands. What if these are his? Maybe I should have just sat there, all casual. But now what do I do? Pretend like I lost a contact?

Oh, right. They don't have contacts yet.

God, this is so stupid!

I try to keep my breathing steady, even though I am terrifyingly close to panting like a dog. He walks up and down the room for what seems like an hour but is probably ten minutes. I can hear him sliding books in and out of the shelves. I will him to just pick up a book and leave with it. If he's looking for these letters, he's not going to find them without finding me.

My knees are starting to ache from kneeling on the thin carpet. Haven't they ever heard of carpet pad?

When he gets to the Shakespeare section near the far window, he pauses. What did I do with that *Hamlet* book? Did I put it back, or did I just set it down on the edge of the shelf?

And then he starts walking toward me. I cover my mouth with my hand to keep from freaking out. Part of me wants to pop to my feet and yell, *Boo!* like it was just a little joke, but somehow I don't think he'll find it funny. Plus, he's probably still pretty mad about the whole breakfast thing earlier today.

I watch his boots pivot slightly, and then he stops moving. What's he looking for? What's he *waiting* for?

But then he turns on his heel and walks out, just in time to keep my lungs from exploding. I heave a big sigh, and then breathe deeply for the first time in ten minutes. My heartbeat returns to normal. My palms are sweaty where I've been gripping the papers.

These letters must be what Alex was after.

I sit up and look around to make sure no one else is in the room.

I'll just take a teensy little peek . . .

9

I flip over the first folded note.

The Duke of Harksbury is all it says on the outside. It's written in a feminine scrawl, little curlicues and elegant loops all over the place.

I know I shouldn't be reading this. It's probably a bunch of love letters. I should just shove it back between the couch and the table and forget about it.

But I got stuck here somehow, and I need to discover everything I can about where I'm staying. There's no telling what kind of clues I could come across if I pay attention. Clues that could lead me back to the twenty-first century.

And okay, I'm a *teensy* bit curious as to whether he has a girlfriend.

I take a deep breath and slide my finger under the fold and open the letter. The same cute penmanship greets me.

Your Grace,

I am certain my previous correspondence has been lost, for I have written you with each passing month, and yet still I receive no reply. Is it so easy to forget all of your whispered promises?

Your daughter was born two months ago.

I jerk backward and the letter flutters from my hand. Alex has a daughter? He's freaking nineteen and he has a daughter?

The world swims as I scramble to put together the pieces. He's not married, is he? Even if he were, this lady is definitely not living here. I mean, I would have seen her by now. Not to mention a two-month-old little baby.

I shake my head. Maybe I shouldn't jump to conclusions . . . .

It pains me to ask for money, but I have no choice. The daughter of a duke should not go hungry, and I fear that is in her future. Please, I will not shame your family or utter a word of this to a soul. There will be no scandal, for no one will know, but I beg of you to help me. I am unable to find work—

I snap the letter shut, suddenly feeling nauseated.

He has a daughter and he abandoned her. And she and her mother are *poor?* He's living in this giant mansion with servants at his beck and call, and his own daughter has nothing?

This is disgusting. Did he sleep with a maid or something and then send her away?

Oh God, he's so much worse than I could have possibly imagined. He's not just an arrogant jerk . . . He's an absolute wretched human being!

I gather up the letters and tie the ribbon back around them, wishing I'd never found them at all. I'll read the rest of the letters later and figure out what to do.

I jump up and swiftly leave the room. I'll deposit the letters somewhere in my bedroom and then finish exploring.

An hour later, I've figured out the layout of Harksbury, but I haven't found a single item to prove my theory of make-believe.

I mean, these people don't even have indoor plumbing. There are chamber pots in most of the bedrooms. For real. And I think I found the laundry room, except they sure don't use washing machines. Forget about the kitchen. It was sweltering in there from actual fires for cooking with, and the servants looked at me with such shocked expressions I backpedaled and fled before they could yell at me for being there.

God, 1815 really stinks. In my century, a girl gets child support if a guy like Alex does something like this. Or a big college fund, in my case, though I would have preferred an actual dad. One who didn't up and move to the East Coast and start a whole new family three years ago, and then invite me out, like that wouldn't be the most awkward summer of my life.

I shake my head and hope it sends the memories flying to the back of my mind, where they belong. At least my dad calls twice a week and pays child support on time.

Alex is such a schmuck, to live like this and have a kid on the side. What a rotten person. And seriously, he's nineteen. That's just wrong.

I reach the bottom of the steps and head down the east wing.

Harksbury seems to be made up in sort of a rectangular fashion, around the courtyard I'd seen earlier. The two main wings come together at the big foyer and grand staircase, and then go off in opposite directions, a good couple hundred feet or more, each hall lined with door after door after door. It'll take me days to open them all, but I don't think I'm going to try because nothing I've found so far has been useful.

Downstairs are a bunch of sitting rooms and dining halls and a few smaller bedrooms. Upstairs are the library and more bedrooms, but those are bigger, some with whole sitting rooms attached to them.

Only parts of the house have hardwood. The rest is carpeted. Everything is bigger than normal, stately and grand. The doors would accommodate a seven-foot guy and the ceilings are so high I could stand on a chair and leap into the air and not be able to touch them.

But it's all sort of cold in its grandiosity. Three people do not need a house this size. Especially since the servants seem to keep to the lower level, except when cleaning.

Which they do a lot of. They're everywhere, dusting and sweeping and beating rugs.

Every time I find another room, another fancy painting, and another oversized piece of furniture, I think about the letters stuffed under my mattress. How could he live like this while his own daughter is living God knows where?

I despise him. I abhor him. I hate him.

I'm mumbling to myself as I exit the house and wander through the gardens. They could still have that private jet back here, right?

I slow as I approach the barns. There's some kind of rhythmic beat coming from inside. It's almost musical.

When I round the corner, I see a man with an overturned bucket tapping away on it with two sticks, like a drummer. Two boys who look barely thirteen are doing the absolute funniest Riverdance I have ever seen, jumping around like happy little leprechauns, their elbows jutting out and their toes barely touching the ground.

I can't stop the laugh that bubbles out of me. I clamp a hand over my mouth but it's too late; they've heard it. One of the boys stops so quickly he falls over and promptly turns beet red.

And now I feel *really* guilty, because I know precisely how the burn in his cheeks feels. The last thing I should be doing is laughing at other people.

"I'm sorry, I don't mean to laugh. I've just, uh, never seen dancing like that before."

The younger boy, a redhead, picks himself up off the ground with a wide-eyed look. "You are American," he says, as if I'm a mythical creature.

I nod. "Yes. And, uh, we have different dances where I come from."

"Can you show us one?" The second boy, a dark-haired kid, steps forward, looking intrigued.

I stifle a laugh. "Oh, uh, no. I'm a horrible dancer."

"Please?" the redheaded boy asks. "I have never seen an American dance."

I just laughed at them thirty seconds ago. Wouldn't that make me mean if I just blow them off now?

"I doubt you'd want to see these dances," I say, stalling. I feel kind of bad. But I really can't dance. I'll make a fool of myself.

"Oh, but I do. Most certainly."

"Oh." Well, then.

I could try, right? Just some tiny little thing?

But what do I share? MC Hammer? The Running Man? The Electric Slide? A little Macarena?

"Uh," I say, stepping forward. "How about, um, the Robot?"

"The Robot?" the two boys ask in unison.

Did the word *robot* even exist in 1815?

"Yeah. You, uh, hold your arms out like this," I say, demonstrating the proper way to stand like a scarecrow. I can't believe I'm doing this. "And then relax your elbows and let your hands swing. Like this."

I'm really not doing it well, but by the way their eyes widen, you'd think I just did a full-on pop-and-lock routine with Justin Timberlake. They mimic my maneuver, making it look effortless.

The drummer guy stands up and gets in on the action, swinging his arms freely. The guy's better than me after a two-second demo. Figures.

"Okay, then, uh, you sort of walk and you try to make everything look stiff and, uh, unnatural. Like this." I show him my best robotic walk, my arms mechanical in their movements.

The two boys and the drummer immediately copy me, and

by the time they've taken four or five steps, they seriously look like robots.

In no time they're improvising, and their laughter trickles up toward the rafters of the barn.

Yeah. That's my cue to leave before inspiration strikes and I try to show them how to break-dance but only succeed in breaking my neck.

I slip out of the barn unnoticed, grinning to myself as I walk the gravel path back toward the house, my skirts brushing the dirt.

At least somewhere, I'm not Callie the Klutz. Even if it's just some smelly old barn.

There's hope for me after all.

10

Once back in my room, I lie on my bed and stare at the ceiling.

I know I should read the letters stuffed under my mattress, but I can't bring myself to dig them out.

They hit too close to home.

That poor little girl is going to grow up without her dad. At least she won't know what she's missing. Me, I had a father for twelve years. And he wasn't such a bad father, either. A little busy most of the time, but not bad.

And then, out of the blue, he left my mom. It's been the two of us ever since. I'm pretty sure she let me go on the London trip because it gave me a convenient excuse for turning down my dad and summer in the Hamptons. I don't have the opportunity to think much more on the subject before the maid comes in, the hardwood floors creaking under her steps.

"I've come te help ye change fer dinner."

I sit up and look at my clothing. It's still clean and relatively wrinkle-free, which is an accomplishment for me. I'm forever dropping food on my clothes. "I'm sure this is fine," I say.

Her mouth tightens like she's fighting a smile. "A mornin' dress is no' suitable fer a dinner party."

"A dinner *party?*" I don't like the sound of that.

She nods as she pulls me over to the stool near the wardrobe. "Yes. 'Er Ladyship invited our neighbors te dine te celebrate yer arrival. Ye could hardly go in such casual wear."

Casual? *This* is casual? Compared to her basic black dress, I'm ready for a night on the town.

She's throwing clothing in my direction and I don't know what I'm supposed to do, so I just catch it and stand there, my arms filling. And when I see the last item, I freeze, holding it between two hands and staring as if it's a typhoid-infested blanket.

In fact, it's worse. It's a *corset.*

She's seriously going to put me in a corset.

"I'm under strict order by the lady o' the house te make ye presentable. Ye'r a guest o' Harksbury and as such, ye must be properly attired." The maid tucks an errant strand of her dark hair behind her ear, as if she's suddenly aware of her own appearance.

I know without asking that those are not her words; I can actually hear the grouchy old lady saying them, even through the maid's thick accent.

I swallow and nod, stepping forward to accept my fate. I sure hope all those girls in historical novels are exaggerating.

I don't exactly have a high pain threshold. I cried the last time I got a filling.

As she laces the corset, and the volume of air inside my lungs depletes, I gain a new appreciation for my ancestors. This sucks. Oh sure, it's not too bad at first. But it's sort of like putting on a pair of shoes that's just a teensy bit too snug. You don't notice it too much for the first ten minutes, but then it becomes so apparent you can't ignore it. It's like a girdle and a push-up bra put together, and I think my boobs must be right under my chin, because there's no room for them in front of my ribs.

Next she pulls me to my feet and puts my arms straight up in the air, like I'm a little kid. She pulls a crimson dress over my head. It's a soft satin, with pretty little rosebuds embroidered along the short puffy sleeves. It's not nearly as scratchy as the peach gown I'd been wearing all morning, so I feel a little better about changing.

Of course, I'd feel a *lot* better if I could breathe, but I guess that's not possible.

She guides me back to the vanity, where her next mission is redoing my braids. My scalp is screaming within ten seconds.

I've got to distract myself somehow. I clear my throat. "So, um, what is your name?"

She pauses. "Eliza, miss."

"Oh. I'm Ca—Rebecca."

Whew, that was close.

"I know, miss."

Oh. Right. Okay then.

"Shouldn't you have today off? Isn't it Sunday?"

"I've a half day off ever' three days. I'll be out temorra afte'noon."

I snort. "A *half* day?"

God, that's ridiculous. She doesn't even get a single full day off? What is Alex, some kind of slave driver? Jeez.

"I've got some slippers that should fit you," she says, ignoring my question. She bends over and slips a pair onto my feet, and my toes sigh in relief. They're soft and comfortable. Thank God. I'd like to look at them more closely, but I can't bend over. This corset is *stiff.*

"Good! Ye are ready. The guests are gatherin' in the drawin' room."

I nod but just stare blankly at her because I don't know where that is. Or rather, *which* room that is, of the dozens I explored. She seems to get my point because she says, "Oh!" and motions me to follow her.

She takes me to the grand staircase and stops at the top, pointing across the foyer to an open door partway down the hall. I can hear voices and laughter trickling out.

I take a tiny, timid step down the stairs, and then another. The pretty red gown is trailing behind me on the steps.

I stop and reach up to check my hair.

Is it hot in here?

I touch my cheeks.

They're warm.

I take three more steps.

I want to turn around but a glance upward reveals that the maid is still standing at the top, staring at me like I'm crazy.

I swallow.

I look good. I know I do. It's a beautiful dress, and my hair is done up like it's supposed to be, and no one here wears name-brand *anything*. Well, except me and my heels.

For the first time in my life, no one knows me as Callie Montgomery, class nerd with a big mouth and two left feet. I can be Callie the popular girl. Callie, the girl everyone likes to talk to and laugh with.

Or, well, Rebecca, the popular girl. Minor technicality.

I force myself to walk naturally down the last dozen steps, my shoulders pulled back and my head held high.

I cross the foyer in what feels like milliseconds, and before I can even pause to take a deep breath, I'm in the drawing room, overcome by the loud buzz of conversation.

So many people. There must be at least fourteen of them, all dressed to the nines like this is a five-star restaurant. They're gathered in groups around the fireplace or the wood-trimmed brocade furniture. I'm grateful Eliza forced me to change because, I now realize, I would have looked ridiculous in that peach dress.

The grumpy old lady wears a cream-colored satin dress that skims over those extra thirty pounds she's sporting and just touches the ground. Her gray hair is twisted up on her head and held together with pins I can't even see. She might look pretty, except her piercing green eyes are narrowed to tiny slits as she listens to one of the guests speak in her ear.

Seriously, if the woman smiled, just once, I'd probably keel over in shock.

Emily is walking toward me, wearing a modest sky-blue dress that makes her skin practically glow as her dark hair shines. Carefully placed ringlets—so different from the messy look Mindy prefers—hang down near her temple and chin, framing her tiny little face. She looks like a china doll. A really pretty one.

My eyes search the room, and I don't realize who I'm looking for until I've spotted him. He's so tall, he's easy to find. He's wearing a black jacket with shiny brass buttons and a snowy-white shirt, complete with some kind of tie that is wrapped all around his neck. He's nodding his head to something someone is saying, and then I catch his eye, and before I can duck, he's staring straight at me.

I clench my jaw and try not to think of the letter I've just read. It makes me want to march right up to him and slap him across the face. Once for that lady, once for the kid, and once for me.

He says nothing. He does nothing. He just stares at me and I stare back, and for a long moment I don't see anything else.

11

The room is spinning but Alex's eyes aren't moving; they're locked on mine. He's probably sending me mental signals to *behave like a good little society girl.*

The moment is broken when Emily tugs on my elbow. "Oh, Rebecca, my gown looks beautiful on you! Much prettier than on myself. You shall keep it," she says.

"Oh, no, I couldn't—" I start, but she waves me away.

"You must."

"Oh," I say.

"Look, Victoria wants us," she says. I cringe when I realize Victoria is the grouchy old lady. Oh, joy.

I follow Emily over to where Victoria is standing. Emily bobs into a curtsy and I awkwardly follow, and then trip on the skirt and have to grab the elbow of a random guy to stop myself from falling.

Victoria stifles a laugh and I want to punch her for it, but the guy distracts me. "You must be Rebecca," he says, in a voice that sounds sweet and intelligent, if a voice can be intelligent.

"Yes, please, uh, excuse me for my clumsiness."

Poor Rebecca. I'm going to single-handedly ruin her reputation before she even gets to England.

He grins widely and his entire face melts into this pleasant look that makes me feel better, like he's not judging me. "Your American accent is charming," he says. I would guess he's close to forty, with gray hair around his temples, and the rest chestnut brown.

"Thank you," I say. And then I curtsy again for some reason, which is absurd and totally unnecessary.

"It's been some time since I've heard tales from America. Dinner should be most intriguing."

Oh, crap. Why didn't I think of this? People will want to know all about America. But the 1815 version of it. Stupid history—why didn't I pay more attention? I'm not even sure how many states existed in 1815.

"Yes, I'd love to . . . regale you with some tales."

I sound ridiculous. I can't tell if I'm talking like they think I should or if I'm talking like *I* think I should, which probably isn't the same thing.

"Was the Atlantic crossing a difficult one?"

I shrug. "No, it was quite smooth really."

Emily chimes in. "We hadn't expected her for nearly four weeks yet. She certainly made good time."

Nearly four weeks? That means less than four. I'll have to remember that. I can't be here when the real Rebecca shows up. That would be a disaster.

"Perhaps you could play a song on the pianoforte? I'm sure our guests would enjoy it," Victoria says.

Great. If the pianoforte is the same thing as the piano, I'm screwed. My mom had wanted me to play but gave up when I was twelve because the only thing I could play was "Chopsticks."

"Oh, I'd so love to hear the number you told me about," Emily says.

To my horror she's looking right at me.

"What?" I say. "I'm not certain I recall what I'd written you about."

"You said it was a beautiful melody and a full ten minutes long. You said it was complicated but pleasing to the ear." She's looking at me with such wide, innocent eyes that I don't know what to say without feeling like a jerk.

"Oh, right." I swallow. Why couldn't Rebecca have been a no-talent hack like me? She's probably perfect at everything. I'm doomed. "I'm sure I exaggerated a bit. I'm sure it would not be of interest to anyone."

Oh God, everyone is staring at me. There must be twenty-eight eyeballs on me right now. This ridiculously large room with all of its oversized furniture feels like an elevator as the walls close in.

"There's no need to be modest, dear," Victoria says. She's pushing me toward the corner of the room. Why hadn't I noticed the piano? Danger! Danger!

"No, really, I can't," I say, trying to push back.

"Do not disappoint our guests, *Rebecca*."

There's a note of anger in Victoria's voice, and it makes me stop cold in my tracks and realize what I'm doing: embarrassing her. In front of her guests. I bet that doesn't fall under *Things a Well-Bred Girl Would Do*. I take a deep breath and just nod at her, racking my brains for some clever way to turn this around, but nothing is coming.

I guess I did snap at her this morning, and now she's throwing this party because of my arrival. This is the least I can do, right? I walk slowly to the piano like I'm walking the plank. This is not going to be good. People are going to go insane if I have to play for a full ten minutes.

Okay then. Piano it is. I hope they like "Chopsticks."

I move to sit at the piano, wishing it was Emily playing instead of me. Or even her sitting beside me and carrying me through this torture.

Wait! That's it!

"Emily? Perhaps the guests would enjoy a duet. I've a simple one I can teach you."

Her eyes widen as she tucks one of her curls behind an ear and looks around, like she can't believe her luck. How cute.

"Really. Come sit. If the guests would enjoy a single player, their enjoyment shall be double with both of us." I'm talking like them now, right? Right?

She nods and practically bounces over to the piano. The girl is like a puppy dog.

We each pull off our gloves and set them on top of the piano. I show her a repetitive set of notes, the lower part of "Heart and Soul," the only other piece I'm good at. If Tom Hanks can pull it off on a giant piano in *Big*, I'm sure Emily can master it.

Once Emily gets a good rhythm going, I pick up the melody on the higher part of the piano. It spans maybe a dozen keys, and I can get away with using a couple fingers for the entire rendition. Exactly the kind of song I can hack. The keys are cool on my skin as I complete the first round, the song filling the room as the crowd falls silent.

The group in the room gathers and watches us, edging closer, and I feel Alex's eyes burning into me. I want to look up at him, but I know I'll foul up on the piano so I don't. I can tell Emily is enjoying herself because she sort of rocks back and forth as she moves up and down the keys, and her smile is so big I can *feel* it.

I nudge Emily into stopping and then trail off with a few keys.

When we finish, I look up and everyone claps. Even Victoria looks pleased. I guess "Heart and Soul" isn't known by everyone over six years old in this era. For one tiny moment, I feel like having everyone stare at me is a good thing, like they like me.

And then I stand and try to scoot the bench back, but Emily is still sitting on it. It's amidst a standing ovation that I fall over backward and crash to the floor.

"Oh, I, uh, oh." In a split second I'm on my feet, waving away the gentleman who has rushed forward to assist me. Wow. My skin must be crimson by this point. I brush any errant dust off my skirts. "Emily? Why don't you play the next one," I say, hoping to divert all the eyes.

She just beams and turns back to the piano. Thank God.

I find a chair nearby and make a hasty retreat. My face cools as I watch Emily, still smiling from ear-to-ear. Her hazel eyes sparkle as her brown curls bounce with enthusiasm. There's some part of her that looks more thirteen than eighteen. A naïve, hopeful streak.

I'm such a schmuck for pretending to be Rebecca. For pretending to be Emily's friend. Because truthfully, I *want* to be her friend. But without the layers of lies between us. They're like a rubber band, pulling and stretching. And it can't last forever. It'll break.

She's going to know. Whether it's because I disappear and end up back in the twenty-first century, or because my lies are uncovered, she's going to know.

And it might make me a coward, but I hope I'm not here to see it.

Emily finishes a lively tune, and the guests clap again.

"You'll make Denworth a fine wife!" one of them says, and I almost choke on my own spit.

Wife?

Emily's smile turns stiff, and the light leaves her eyes.

Now she looks eighteen.

"Thank you," she says.

I grind my teeth together. What's going on here?

"Have you written him, as I asked?" Victoria says, stepping toward the piano.

"Not yet," Emily says.

Just as Victoria opens her mouth to speak again, Emily picks up another tune, up-tempo and loud, and it drowns out whatever Victoria had meant to say.

It's clear Emily doesn't want to speak of the Denworth situation with Victoria.

But I have to know what's going on—something's not adding up. Emily should be happy about an engagement, if that's what's happening.

Tomorrow, I'll get to the bottom of this.

12

When I get up the next morning, I hurry to breakfast, which is served in the sunroom, a much smaller room than we'd dined in last night.

I'm glad we're somewhere else. I don't want to remember the absolute disaster of dinner the night before.

It all started when a servant walked into the drawing room after my piano-playing debut and said dinner was served. I'd skipped lunch in order to explore Harksbury, so naturally I was hungry. So I got up and headed to the dining room.

Except I was the only one. Everyone else assembled in pairs, and I got stuck at the end with an elderly guy who was most definitely not as rich as the others. And as we followed the parade into the dining room, I realized we were placed in order of *importance*.

One guess who was at the back.

Me. Now why did that feel just like high school? So much for this dinner supposedly being in my honor! Not that I wanted that much of the spotlight, but still.

It went downhill from there. I talked to the servants again. Yeah, that's most *definitely* a faux-pas. You could have heard a pin drop when I asked if they had ketchup. And then I stuck a knife in my mouth to eat a piece of chicken. Faux-pas number two. Oh and apparently I was supposed to hold a piece of bread in one hand and the fork in the other while eating fish. Faux-pas number three.

I seriously could not keep up with them and barely made it out alive.

This morning, I'm relieved to see Emily at the table, quietly eating alone. At least I can do everything wrong and she won't care.

There aren't any servants around, so I just dig into the ham and fruits available on the sideboard. "So, uh, no bacon?" I joke. They always seem to prepare way more food than we could ever eat.

These people have never heard the word *moderation* before.

Emily looks up from her plate. "Victoria—er—Her Grace believes bacon is for the lower class."

"Oh," I say, not sure how I'm supposed to respond. It seems kind of weird to decide we can have ham and not bacon, but whatever. I don't get anything in this century. I take my plate and sit down at the table across from Emily. The summer sun is already streaming through the windows. It must be at least ten or eleven. I've given up keeping track of time here; they seem to run on their own clock.

The room falls silent again. "So, Emily," I say.

She's been pushing her food around for ten minutes, and when I break the silence, she looks up as if she's forgotten I was even in the room.

"This fiancé of yours . . . have you mentioned him before? I don't recall." Do I sound casual? I hope so.

She shakes her head and then looks back at her plate. What happened to happy, bubbly Emily—the one I've come to know and like? The one who is part-girl, part-puppy dog?

"No. We've only just become engaged."

"Where did you meet?"

"At his estate, after my father arranged it."

I don't like where this is headed. "Why did your father arrange it?"

Her voice is flat. "For the marriage, of course."

I *really* don't like where this is headed. "You don't mean . . . he introduced you to him so that he could . . . *arrange your marriage*, do you?" I know I sound really dense, but I've never encountered a real, live arranged marriage. I thought they were mythical. Sort of like unicorns.

She just nods, but I see her swallow, and I wonder if she has a lump in her throat like I do. She's looking down, but I don't think she sees anything on her plate. Has she blinked? At all?

"And . . . do you like him?"

She sets down her fork. "He is . . . an agreeable sort of man. With great wealth. I shall want for nothing," she says. But it sounds ridiculous. It's like she's reading off cue cards.

I shift in my chair. It's suddenly hard and uncomfortable. "But do you love him?"

"I shall want for nothing," she repeats. Her eyes are a little shinier than they were thirty seconds ago. She picks up her fork, but her hand trembles a little bit when she grips it too hard.

"Emily . . . you can be honest with me. We're friends."

Even as the words leave my mouth, I want to take them back. Emily is such a nice girl, and here I am, lying straight to her face, over and over. Betraying her trust as I masquerade as her friend.

Yet somehow even though I know she's friends with *Rebecca*, I kind of feel like we're friends too. There's just something about her that makes me trust her, even as I do nothing to earn *her* trust.

That's when the waterworks start. She blinks several times, but the tears still escape and leave shiny, salty trails down her perfectly round cheeks. "I could never love him. He is callous and rude. He is thirty years my senior and quite set in his ways," she says, her voice quivering.

Thirty years older? He's ancient!

My jaw hangs open as I stare at her. She drops her fork with a clatter and picks up a napkin and dabs at her eyes, staring toward the ceiling. The cracks in her happy façade are spreading, and I think she's about to completely crumble.

"Does your father know how you feel?"

She nods. "Yes. I've pleaded with him, but he will not be swayed. I think he tired of hearing my appeals, and that's why he sent me to stay for two months at Harksbury. It is his wish that I will return home at peace with his decision."

This is so wrong, on so many levels. I can't even get words to come out of my mouth because there are too many spinning around in my head. Everything I come up with is empty and stupid.

1815 is *so* screwed up. First the secret daughter Alex has . . . now an arranged marriage? Could things get any more twisted?

I've landed in Regency England: 90210. Just as much drama; a lot less glamour.

Emily wipes her nose with a napkin and inhales deeply. "I was so pleased to see you when you arrived. You are so smart and independent; I just knew when you arrived early that it was a gift to me. You are my dearest friend, Rebecca. You must help me."

Oh, wow, I feel like such a jerk right now. The real Rebecca is probably brilliant and would know just what to say in this situation. She'd probably have a hundred plans for things to do, and she'd launch right into action and find Emily a way to freedom.

I can see it on Emily's face. She's looking at me with such hope, like I'll fix everything. She wants nothing to do with whoever this Denworth guy is. And I know in this moment, whatever I do, I have to get her out of it. I owe it to her.

It's what Rebecca would do. So it's what I must do.

Wait—what if it's what I am *supposed* to do? What if it's the reason I'm here? What if somehow breaking Emily's engagement is my *mission?* My purpose? I found myself in Rebecca's shoes so I'd be in a position to assist Emily.

If I do this, it could fix everything. And if it doesn't, well, then I'll try something else. There's got to be a reason someone from the twenty-first century is stuck in 1815, right? It's so I can assert my modern sensibilities and fix some things.

"Don't worry, Emily. I'll help you. We'll break your engagement."

I don't know what I'm doing. I don't know how I'm supposed to help her.

But I know I have to. I just have to develop a plan.

Immediately.

13

I am in heaven. Well, as close to heaven as you can get in 1815. After watching what must have been eight different servants bring bucket after bucket of hot water up to my room, I have a full tub of gloriously warm water to soak in. And I'm not leaving until it's cold and I'm all wrinkly.

There's some kind of scented oil in the water, and if I didn't believe in aromatherapy before, I do now. This is the most relaxed I've been in over forty-eight hours.

Since I didn't get to go to the club with Angela, Mindy, and Summer, I'm going to make up for it tonight, Regency-style at the Pommeroy dance. I'll dress to the nines and flirt with some hot guys, and have the time of my life.

When the water gets too cold to tolerate, I get out and put on a cotton nightgown the maid left out for me. Emily insisted that we get ready for the dance together, which is probably a good thing—I need major help figuring out what I'm supposed to wear to something like this.

I've never even been asked to homecoming. Tonight will probably be the first time I ever actually dance with a guy. Crazy. I had to travel two hundred years to go to a freaking dance.

But whatever. I'm going to make the most of it and dance the night away, even if I am wearing weird clothes and they don't play any music I recognize.

I grab a string that disappears into a hole in the wall. It's supposed to connect with a bell somewhere and tell Eliza that I need her. I can't hear it, so I just have to assume it's ringing in some far-off land. I heard Emily once call it 'below stairs,' but I have no idea which stairs she was talking about.

In any case, it must work because Eliza arrives a few minutes later and immediately sets to work on my wet hair, combing and putting it into little rags that are supposed to help give it a curl, until there are so many they're piled all over my head. I feel very fifties retro when she's done.

"Aren't you supposed to be off today?" I ask.

"I was, miss. The whole afte'noon."

I scrunch my brow. "Well, I think you should take tomorrow off too. If anyone has a problem with that, send them to me."

She looks confused, like this has to be a trick.

"You deserve a day off. Don't worry."

"Yes, miss," she says, suddenly looking very, very happy.

"Just promise me you'll sleep in," I say.

Her lips curl into a smile as she curtsies. "Yes, miss."

"Great. Well, I think you can go. I'm going to be getting ready over in Emily's chambers."

As soon as she's gone, I'm ready to go to Emily's room. I walk toward the door in my cotton nightgown, but stop halfway there. It seems . . . bizarre to leave the room like this. I'm wearing a thin nightdress that barely covers my butt. I haven't seen my bra since day one, so until I get the corset back on, I can't possibly walk out my bedroom door.

I stare at the bell pull again, wondering if I should call back Eliza and ask her for something else to put on. And directions to Emily's. Why hadn't I thought of any of this before I sent her away?

But I feel kind of bad, bugging her so much. I'm not used to having someone at my beck and call. It's kind of weird. So the only solution is to grab one of the blankets off my bed. I look silly, but I wrap it around my body until I look like a big burrito.

Yeah. Modest. That's me.

I peek out my door and look both ways. No one is around.

I'm pretty sure Emily said her room is in the opposite wing, and that if I take this back staircase, I can get there without going by the front entry.

That works great in theory, except Harksbury really is bigger than my high school and I get lost. I'm pretty sure I pass the same creepy portraits three times. I think their eyes might be following me, like in Scooby-Doo. I even think I take the servants' stairs at some point, because they're narrow and lit only by a single small window, so there's no way Victoria or Alex would take them. Alex probably wouldn't even fit, he's so tall. It's good I won't run into them, because hobbling around wrapped in a blanket like this, I look like a complete buffoon. A half-naked, burrito buffoon.

At some point I realize I've made it to the opposite wing. I spot the courtyard through a set of leaded glass windows and the view is the opposite of the one I've seen from my wing. Thank God. It would have been terrible to wander much longer, looking like I do. I could have run into—

Alex.

Alex!

Just seeing him makes my anger boil.

He's staring at me, his mouth slightly agape, his eyes wide. Is it me, or is he blushing? Hasn't he ever seen a burrito-girl before? Or is it these dead-sexy rag curlers in my hair that only an old lady would wear? Not only am I a burrito, I'm a geriatric one. Fabulous.

"Uh, I'm looking for Emily's room," I say. I tighten my grip on the blanket, hoping none of me is hanging out anywhere it shouldn't be.

He doesn't speak, just motions me to follow him. I walk beside him, the blanket dragging behind me. There are about a thousand things I'd like to say to him right now—Eliza's pitiful schedule, that poor lady's letters—but I can't possibly have a serious conversation looking like this, so I don't say any of them.

When we get to the door, it's open, and he steps aside so I can enter. He's so close to the door that I end up brushing past him when I go by.

"Thanks," I mutter. As an afterthought I curtsy, but I'm not sure he can even tell because the blanket just sort of mushrooms out. I scurry through the door and slam it behind me, and then fall against it. Alex is probably staring right at the door in his face. Bet he doesn't get *that* every day. It almost makes me feel better.

"Oh. My. God. I'm a walking disaster," I say to Emily.

She's sitting on a stool, wearing a gorgeous yellow robe, and spins around to look at me.

A robe. Now why couldn't I have had one of those?

"What is the matter?" She's wearing little rag-curlers, like me, but on her they look cute and perky. The white cloth contrasts with her dark locks, like some kind of fashion statement. Somehow I doubt I look quite as charming.

I walk over to her bed and throw myself on it with a heavy sigh. "I just walked around wrapped up like this and ran into Alex. God, I'm lucky I didn't see anyone else. I bet Victoria would have just *loved* seeing me like this."

Emily giggles. "You do look quite silly."

"Thanks," I say, rolling over on the bed. "I can't believe he saw me."

Emily sips at a small glass on her vanity and then turns and stares right into my eyes. "I had believed you had no interest in my cousin."

I snarl my lip at her in disgust. "Oh, I am so not interested in him. *He* is only interested in *himself*. I mean, really. Could he show *some* interest and compassion for the people around him? He's totally self-centered. And on top of that, he thinks I should censor everything I say and be a docile little girl or something. I mean, *really*."

Her grin widens. "There is no need to sway me. I believe you."

"Oh."

So then why is she grinning at me like that?

And more importantly, why doesn't she hate him like I do? I mean, she might not know about the secret kid, but she knows he's all for her marrying that Denworth guy because he's done nothing to help her get out of it. Shouldn't she resent him, even if he *is* her cousin?

"Now, let us talk of more important topics: our attire for tonight's dance."

And now I grin back at her and all thoughts of Alex disappear. This is going to be *so* fun.

14

She gets up and walks to a row of armoires. Yes, there's more than one. She throws open several doors, revealing dress after dress after dress. I'm surprised they're not on hangers, though . . . They're folded neatly, each with its own little shelf.

My grin gets bigger with each door. This is like shopping. Only better, because I trust Emily's fashion sense more than my own.

"My father believed it important that I wear the latest fashions in order to secure a match with Denworth. While I hardly agreed with the cause, I certainly had fun procuring more gowns."

I think she might get all sniffly about it again, but she doesn't seem concerned as she buries herself in a heap of gowns.

"I think we'd best wear muslin. Though this is but a country-dance, we'd do well to observe the fashions from last season. Hm, but I do have many other gowns that would suit you nicely." She pauses, tapping a finger on her tiny dimpled chin. "Perhaps we shall forego the muslin for tonight after all."

She lost me at muslin. I don't know what she's trying to say, but whatever it is, she's totally into it. She's probably 1815's version of a fashionista.

"Last season?" Is she talking like, *the spring collection* or something? They could not possibly have runways in this century.

"Oh, dear, have you forgotten how much you'd looked forward to your first season? Are you to say you do not *have* a season in America?"

The blank look on my face must convey my confusion.

"Your *coming out*. It would have been last year, as mine was. We'd once wanted to have our first season together, do you not recall? We'd spoken of it often, back then."

"Oh! Yes, um, I do . . . recall. I'd just forgotten. Temporarily. I remember now though." Oh God, there I go rambling again, "So, uh, was it everything you'd hoped it would be?"

Emily is rifling through the dresses, practically buried in them as she tosses them over her shoulders, but when I ask her this, she stands up and turns to look at me, a wide grin and sparkling eyes transforming her face. Wow. She looks . . . ecstatic.

How could anyone force a girl like this to marry some grouchy old guy? I have *got* to figure out a way to help her.

"'Twas amazing. The parties, the dancing, the mingling . . . I wished it would never end." And then, for emphasis, she discards the dresses, stands, and twirls about the room, dancing to a silent melody, her robe floating around her, her curlers flying about her face. She looks positively ethereal. Sometimes this girl is just too adorable.

I don't want to ask why it ended because I'm afraid it has something to do with Denworth. Or maybe it really is just a "season" like she said, and it's only a certain time each year.

"Do you remember how we'd fantasized about Almacks?" She stops spinning long enough to gauge my reaction. My expression must give me away again, because she elaborates. "The exclusive club in London. Only the elite are admitted."

"Oh, right. How could I have forgotten?"

She smiles and crosses the room, plopping down on the bed beside me and lying back. We're so close our curlers nearly touch. I know this should feel weird or awkward or something, but it just feels comfortable. Like Emily is a real friend.

And I haven't had one of those in a year, since Katie left.

"Well, it turns out that Almacks was not nearly as glamorous as I'd hoped. The rooms were quite bare of ornamentation, and the refreshments were terrible. It was all of little consequence, though, for I was allowed a waltz with the Earl of Grant, and caused my very own scandal in the process."

I smile as she talks. I can't help it. She's bubbling with excitement about the entire thing, and it's spilling over and rubbing off on me. I have no idea how a waltz caused a scandal, but it sounds sort of cool.

"The patronesses, of course, were quite a snobbish bunch, and if I should never see them again, I would not be disappointed."

Still no clue what she's talking about. What's a patroness?

I clear my throat. Emily is so into this conversation she could go on all night. And I have to get this out of the way. "So, um, your engagement . . ." Hm. I'm not totally sure what I plan on saying, but I have to broach the subject. "Do you have any, uh, ideas?"

"Ideas?" She sits up and looks at me, one eyebrow raised.

"Yes. Like, on how to break the engagement."

Her face falls. "No, I'm afraid—well, I just don't think it can be done. That's why I was so excited about you . . ." Her voice trails off, and then her face crumples into a frown as the light in her eyes dims.

"Oh, don't worry," I say in a rush. "I've got tons of ideas. I just wanted to see if you had any too. So we could, you know, combine forces." I fight the urge to grimace as I spout yet another lie.

How many have there been, now? I've lost count.

She smiles at me, and it makes my stomach twist. She shouldn't trust me like this.

"Truly? What do you have in mind?"

"Oh, it's too soon to say. Perhaps we can discuss it further tomorrow or the next day."

Lies. All lies.

"Yes, that sounds wonderful. Let's—"

She stops talking when someone knocks on the door. *Thank God.*

"You may enter," Emily calls, all official-like. A servant pokes her head in, followed by my maid, Eliza.

"We've come to help you dress," the first girl says. I think she must be the maid assigned to Emily.

Emily tells her to get us in our "undergarments," and then we shall try out several dresses in order to find one we like.

We sit beside one another on stools while our maids lace our corsets. I can't believe I'm really going to wear this stupid thing again. How am I supposed to dance if I can hardly breathe? Not to mention I found out there is actual whale bone in it, and that's sort of gross. And sad. For the whales, I mean.

When the corset is deemed tight enough (as in, "Oh look, her lungs are the size of peanuts!"), the two maids mumble something about a petticoat, which I think must be the gown thing that goes over the corset. It's softer than I'd expected, which comes as a relief. I'll take comfort anywhere I can get it.

Finally, I'm allowed to look at the actual dresses. There are so many to choose from: blues, greens, reds, and even whites. Some are cotton, some a sleek satin . . . I'm in heaven. I walk around the room in my bare feet, but a few Oriental-style rugs are enough to keep my toes from getting too cold.

What's weird is that I think the rugs really are Oriental, and handmade. They're beautiful and colorful, and I finally get why they came into fashion. Not the cheesy fifty dollar ones at a super store, but elaborate, elegant, *beautiful* rugs.

Emily holds out a navy gown in my direction, then scrunches up her nose and puts it back. For a second I think she's going to hand me a yellow gown with white sleeves, but then she puts that one back too.

Then her face lights up and she pulls out one of the white ones.

"Oh, no, see I'm not good with white," I say, cringing. "I swear to you, I'll spill something all over myself."

"But with your blonde hair and fair skin, it shall make you look angelic," she says.

Angelic? There's a word no one's ever used to describe me. I somehow doubt angels are as klutzy as I am. But okay, I'll try it on.

The maid gets it over my curler-clad head, and I have to admit the dress seems to fit. The little cap sleeves are sort of cute, even if they are a bit puffy. There's a thick, dusty-rose ribbon just under the bustline, and my maid ties a bow behind me. The ribbon is so long it almost reaches the hemline in the back, sort of like its own miniature train. She hands me a pair of elbow-length white gloves, and without even seeing myself, *I know* I look amazing, and pulled together, and perfect.

And judging by the grin on Emily's face, she thinks so too.

She turns back to her armoire, trying to decide on something for herself. She settles on a pretty mint green gown with a low neckline accentuated by sparkling beads. I guess she's feeling a little daring.

Our maids remove our curlers and begin the long process of giving us fancy updos to rival the most expensive salons in the twenty-first century. A marvel, really, considering they have no hair spray.

"So, um, anything I should know about these dance things? I mean, I'm sure you guys do things differently than we do in

America. What should I talk about? I need a primer. Like a list of dos and don'ts."

I cringe when Eliza rips at my hair. Emily's maid seems to be all gentle—why do I get the one with the desire to make me bald?

I can only see Emily in my peripheral vision, but I can tell she's smiling. She's really into this society stuff. "First, you must know that when you arrive, if a gentleman asks you to dance, you must say yes unless you intend to sit out."

"Even if he's a total skeez?" She's silent. I can't turn my head to see her expression. "I mean, uh, even if I don't want to?"

"If you should decline the first man who asks you, it means you have no intention of dancing and no other gentleman shall ask."

"Oh. I get it." No one has *ever* asked me to dance, so I doubt this is going to be a problem. "Anything else?"

My butt is starting to hurt already from this hard stool I'm sitting on, but I'm afraid to move and wrinkle the gown.

"It is not polite to speak of the war, politics, or money. Gossip is always a safe topic."

Okay, *gossip* is a safe topic? How funny is that? I don't bother reminding her I don't *know* any gossip.

"I shall point out Lady Pommeroy to you on our arrival. She may be calling some of the dances, so you'll need to follow her lead—or whoever is the lead couple—when the time is appropriate. She favors the country-dance, though that is not to say she will not intersperse a Scottish reel if it would please her guests."

I just keep nodding to everything she's saying, even though only half of it makes sense.

Actually, who am I kidding? None of it makes sense.

"I believe we are ready!" she says, all too soon.

My maid picks up a small hand mirror and holds it out to me. When I see my reflection, I'm so shocked my jaw drops.

I'm . . . beautiful. My hair is pulled up in a dozen different twists and pinned with little pearl-studded hairpins. Curls cascade down my shoulders.

I look . . . Wow. I stand up but manage to knock over a comb, and it clatters to the ground.

I try to pick it up but can't. The corset means I can lean forward but I can't bend. Eliza nods and scoops it up, as if this isn't odd at all.

I smile and look over at Emily. Tonight . . . it's going to be different. *I'm* going to be different. I'm wearing a corset and a dress and gloves and my Prada heels—which, although a little banged up, have been cleaned and polished to perfection— and I'm going to a ball. Or, er, a dance. Emily says it's only a ball if there are more than five hundred people.

But I can do this. I'm Rebecca. I'm smart and charming and outgoing. Everyone loves an American with stories to tell. I can be that girl. Tonight, I *will* be.

15

Alex is sitting on a stool in a small room near the entry, the double doors propped open. He doesn't see us; he's just staring into the glowing embers of the fire, his hands clasped in his lap.

I stop in the hall, taking the opportunity to stare at him, even though I'm sure Emily will tease me about it later. She's insane if she thinks I actually like him. I just like *looking* at him. The second he opens his mouth, the appeal is gone. And the more I learn about him, the more I despise him. He doesn't care about anyone—not Emily, not his own kid, not his servants.

Today, he's ditched the leather riding boots for some fancy shoes and tall socks. And I *should* think that looks totally lame. I mean, the socks go practically to his knees. His snug pants are navy blue. I can't see the front of his matching jacket, but from behind I can tell that it fits him. *Really well.* In fact, his whole outfit looks like a second skin. It's a shame he's such a complete jerk, or he'd be a great catch.

When he spots us, he stands and leaves the fireplace. Now that he's facing us, I can see he's wearing one of his white neckcloths, tied and looped until his whole neck is covered. His vest is a blue and silver paisley pattern, with buttons just as shiny as his shoes. But what I'm really drawn to is his face—that strong jaw, those burning eyes. His strides are long and purposeful, and before I can inhale a last calming breath, he's in front of us.

"Good evening," he says, and then bows.

Emily and I do our best curtsies.

"Evening," she says.

"Evening," I say, even though at this point it sounds completely redundant.

"Are we quite ready? The landau is waiting."

He emphasizes the *waiting*, like Emily and I are running late. Whatever.

Emily nods, and so I do.

By now I've figured out they never call a carriage just "the carriage," but by the specific name for each one. I'm pretty sure the more carriages you have, the richer you are. Emily said once that the Earl of Porth could not afford to "keep a carriage" because of his gambling habits, as if that were deplorable.

So I'm guessing since Alex has something like eight carriages, he's pretty rich. I've also realized my original estimate of servants was way, *way* off. I've come to the conclusion that there are at least forty. Maybe fifty.

I wonder if *any* of them get real weekends.

As we walk toward the front door, Emily does her best to embarrass me. "I've loaned Rebecca the dress she is wearing. Doesn't it look beautiful on her?"

Oh God, really? She had to go there? I don't understand why she doesn't totally hate him. He obviously doesn't care about *us*.

The expression on his face is still the perma-blank look he's been sporting since the moment I met him, but he turns to stare at me, his piercing green eyes cutting right through me. And so I stare back, even as my cheeks heat up to the point where my whole face must look like a red tomato. So much for my fair skin.

I don't even think he's going to say anything. But then he speaks. "Yes. She looks lovely," he says. And I swear—by the tone of his voice, it sounds like he might actually mean it.

Emily nods. "Are we ready?"

The three of us walk out the enormous front doors as a carriage is pulling around, the horses' hooves clattering on the rocks. This particular carriage is apparently a convertible because the benches are in open air, and I see folded black fabric behind the seats, which might work as a roof if you pulled them up. The doors have some kind of crest or coat of arms painted on them.

This carriage, with gleaming silver all over it, is more decked out than the last one I rode in. It's being pulled by the glossiest horses I've ever seen; they look like brand new pennies. There are two servants in the front seat, dressed in Harksbury's standard-issue black uniform. One of them jumps off before the wheels have even stopped turning and pulls out a step. The other just sits atop his seat, holding the horses steady. One of the horses prances in place, the harness jingling. The whole thing is rather elaborate and grand.

Alex escorts me to the carriage, and I'm hyperconscious of how close he is. He steps to the side of the door and offers me his arm to climb in. I notice how the cuff of his jacket is turned over his hand; his knuckles almost disappear into the sleeve, and there's another shiny brass button near his wrist. Yes, his jacket definitely costs more than anything I own—even my shoes.

He's standing there with his face turned upward and such an arrogant look in his eyes that I flirt with the idea of ignoring his hand and climbing in on my own, but I don't want to anger him. So I rest my gloved hand momentarily on his fingertips and pretend I don't feel the hot tingles shooting up my arm at his touch.

Why is he being nice? Is he doing this because that's who he is, or is this one of those *required* things for guys of his . . . rank?

Emily climbs up and sits on the bench beside me. Alex sits across from us, and all at once the air is sticky and a little too heavy. We can't ignore one another when we're staring right at each other.

But who wants to talk to a guy like him?

The open carriage is a little breezy, and yet still warm. Emily and I are wearing velvet fur-lined capes over our gowns. Mine is a pretty pink color, the same shade as the ribbon under my chest.

I try to think of something smart and witty to say to prove I'm brilliant, but nothing comes to mind. By the time we've pulled out of the big iron Harksbury gates, no one has spoken a word.

Emily breaks the silence. "The sky was such a pleasing shade of blue today. Don't you think?"

I smile and nod. "Yes, it certainly was."

"Why do you suppose the sky is blue? Why not green or red?"

I shrug and follow her gaze. The sun has almost set, the pale blue of day transforming into dark velvet. "It has to do with the light waves. Blue scatters differently than red does."

Emily looks at me quizzically. "You say such odd things at times, Rebecca."

I smile, a little embarrassed. I probably shouldn't show my nerdy side unless under duress. I'm pretty sure there's a rule about that in the *Social Climber's Guide to Regency England.*

"What is this you speak of?" Alex's voice is so deep and unexpected I jerk my eyes from the stars and look at him.

"I'm sorry?"

"The light waves. What do you mean by them?"

Oh. Right. "Um, well, light comes from the sun in waves. Of color. And then they reflect on different things in the atmosphere and . . . Oh never mind."

It's sort of stupid to explain the whole thing, given how complicated it is.

Alex looks straight at me for a long moment, and then turns back to stare at the sky. "And who told you such a thing?"

I snort. "People *much* smarter than you."

"I'm smarter than you think," he says, avoiding my eyes. It's almost dark out. What is he even looking at?

"And I'm not as ignorant as *you* think," I say.

He turns so abruptly I'm surprised he doesn't strain his neck. His jaw tightens, but he doesn't say anything.

I dare him to disagree. I wait for it. But then he just turns away.

Emily breaks the tension. "Do you suppose Denworth will be at the dance?"

Her voice is hardly a whisper, but I hear the hope behind her words anyway. The hope that her future husband is miles and miles away.

"Does he live near here?" I ask.

"Perhaps an hour's ride beyond Harskbury. I do hope he is not in attendance."

Alex stops staring at the passing greenery long enough to look at Emily. "It would do you well to accept the engagement," he says in a scolding voice. Who does he think he is, Emily's father? They're *cousins*. That doesn't give him any authority over her.

"Yes, Your Grace," she says, in a meek voice.

"Why?" I blurt out, before I can stop.

He looks up at me. "Because it is her duty to do her father's bidding."

"And her husband's after that, I suppose?"

"Of course," he says.

"And when is she to do *her own* bidding?"

Alex appears at a loss for words. He blinks those thick lashes a couple of times, but says nothing.

Fortunately, I have enough to say for both of us. Why is it that I can't defend myself to three pretty girls from my class, but when it comes to Emily, I'm as fierce as a lioness with cubs? Or is it Alex who brings this side out? "Emily deserves the same rights as you do. She should be able to choose for herself."

He crosses his arms, looking all the more pompous by the second. "You believe a woman should have the same rights as a man? Is that truly how it is in America?"

"Yes! And if you cared even the tiniest bit about your own blood relation, you'd do something!" Even as I say the words, I don't know who I'm talking about anymore: Emily or Alex's daughter.

He stares me down, his eyes turning even darker. It stops me cold and the anger ebbs, replaced by the realization I've been much too bold. The piercing look freaks me out. Does he know that I know about the letters? "Everyone has a place in society. It would do you good to observe yours."

And then, as if to say the conversation is over, he turns to look toward the passing forest.

It's going to be a long night.

16

The carriage rolls up to the front steps of a mansion almost as big as Alex's. It doesn't have the same round window bays, or quite the same elegant flair, but it's still made of stone, and it's bigger than the biggest mansions I've ever seen back home. The long drive is lined on both sides with hundreds of glowing lanterns. Our driver circles the horses near the front. Before we can stop, there are three more carriages behind us.

Is it insane if I'm proud of how much fancier our carriage looks than the others? Many of them are only pulled by one or two horses—ours has four. I think that means something.

And I think I'm getting this whole elitist-society thing. I'm betting a duke is the equivalent of a star quarterback. So that makes Alex rich, hot, *and* powerful. And he's like my date. Well okay, not really, but if this were a high school prom, I'd so pretend he was. Plus, in my fantasies, he doesn't have a stick up his butt.

There must be a hundred horses and just as many people

decked out in what I'm guessing are the latest fashions: empire waistlines, fur collars, flashy colors, shiny satin—the whole nine. All the men are in suits with shiny polished shoes and even shinier buttons. The colors and styles look more like a Bollywood movie than the subdued shades of Alex's apparel. He looks like he's going to a funeral; they look like they're ready to party.

The tiny bit of relaxed posture Alex sported in the carriage disappears into a rigid spine and an upturned nose. It really *is* possible for him to look even more uptight. Emily takes one of his arms and I realize I'm supposed to take the other. I sigh and wrap my fingers around his elbow. His arm stiffens under my touch, and I wonder if that means escorting me up the steps is a total chore.

Why does that bother me? The guy is a jerk, even if all this gentlemanly pomp is sort of . . . well . . . charming.

The second I remember the letters, though, any sense of charm evaporates. I know what it's like to grow up without a dad around. Whoever that kid is doesn't deserve that. And Alex is here, at a dance, instead of helping his family out. There's nothing charming about blowing off your responsibilities.

As soon as we're inside the doors, I see a dozen servants in powdered wigs lined up, accepting jackets. I untie my cape and turn around, and one of them slips it over my shoulders, then does the same for Emily. We follow a steady flow of people down a long, wide corridor. Both sides are lit up with so many candles that the entire corridor glows in a wash of yellow, the light dancing as we pass. The hum of conversation is like electric energy, and I'm suddenly buzzing with adrenaline. At the end of the hallway there are two doors propped open, and when I step inside, I'm so awed by the scene that I drop my hand from its place at the crook of Alex's elbow. He is quickly pulled into conversation with a man and woman to my left, but I'm frozen in place.

I'm in a ballroom. It must be as big as the gym in my high school, and *way* fancier, with white columns supporting a high ceiling with dozens of coffered squares. There are powder-blue curtains everywhere along the walls, gathered and draped with gold-tasseled sashes. A veranda in one corner holds a band; their lively music drifts over the guests.

Chandeliers and sconces hang everywhere, hundreds of flames casting a romantic glow over the crowd below. The marble floor is glossy and covered by nearly two hundred people, most of them dancing in what, to my horror, appears to be a choreographed routine. They're standing in a row, do-si-doing around one another, clapping hands, and spinning.

I just stare, remembering what Emily had said about a country-dance and a reel, and realizing she'd meant *line dances*.

"I—" I'm about to explain that I have no idea what all this is about when someone walks up to Emily.

He's sort of cute. A little older, like maybe twenty or so, but tall and athletic, with sandy blonde hair and sparkling blue eyes. Unlike Alex's attire, this guy's is colorful: a bright blue jacket with burgundy stripes, and a matching burgundy neckcloth tied in large, lazy twists. His eyes twinkle as he grins, as if the world is at his feet and he couldn't be happier.

I decide immediately that I like him.

He stares straight at Emily as she smiles back. "Miss Thorton-Hawke, it is lovely to see you," he says with a deep bow.

She curtsies back, so low her knees practically touch the ground, and her mint-green dress mushrooms out around her. "The pleasure is mine," she says, in a singsong voice I hardly recognize.

"Save the next dance for me?"

She nods, and then he smiles and disappears into the crowd. For a second I wonder if she's just following her own rule about accepting the first request to dance, but then I realize it's far more than that.

As soon as he's out of earshot, she squeals and grabs my hand. "Oh, I'd hoped he would be here!"

I cock an eyebrow at her.

"His name is Trent Rallsmouth. We met at a country-dance. He is the son of a wealthy merchant and the subject of my greatest adoration."

I want to say something to her, but no words come as I stare into her shining eyes. Trent. That's it. My solution. Somehow, someway, he's the guy she should be with.

Not Denworth. It has to be Trent.

If I fail, it's not just about her being stuck with Denworth— it's about her being without Trent. I'll be denying her a smile like this one forever.

I won't let that happen. Not when I promised her. Not when fixing this could lead me home. "So, what's the deal?"

Emily gives me a blank look.

"What I'm asking is . . . you and Trent . . . are the feelings mutual?"

"I am not certain. I believe so." She looks away for a silent moment and then sighs. "According to my father, it does not matter, for I am betrothed to another . . . more *appropriate* match. He has said that Trent is below me, and he refuses to allow me to marry anyone other than a gentleman."

I swallow and stare into the crowd like it will somehow show me the right words to say, but I end up just standing there, silent. How am I going to fix this?

The evening was supposed to be fun, and now it's turning complicated. Emily's betrothal just became real. The pain she's going to feel . . . It's real. I *have* to do something.

And on top of all that, I don't know these dances! And as soon as the next dance starts, I'm going to be standing here alone while Emily dashes off to dance with Trent. It's like my worst nightmare, come to life.

Turns out 1815 isn't so different from the twenty-first century, because this is *exactly* what would happen if I were back home. Even pretending I'm Rebecca hasn't fixed it.

Why did I think it would change? Flying thousands of miles to Europe didn't change my fate. Traveling two hundred years, it seems, didn't change it either.

17

I chew on my lips as I scan the crowd. There's quite a mix of people here: men and women, boys and girls (though none of them appear to be younger than fourteen). Judging by their clothing alone, some are quite wealthy, and others . . . not so much. And yet none of them seem to care, because they're laughing and dancing and smiling, and I want so badly to be a part of that.

Why can't I? Why do I always do this? My skin tingles with the desire to step outside myself, to walk onto the floor and push away *old* Callie.

But I don't know how. I'll just do something classic like trip on my dress or bump into everyone else. I'm too freaked about the prospect to force myself onto the floor.

There's a crowd of people near the edge of the dance floor, and I squint to see what they're all looking at. And then someone pushes through the group, and to my utter shock I realize it's Alex they all want. They stare longingly after him as he tries to extract himself from the mix.

And they're all girls. Is he supposed to be considered a major catch or something? They must not know what a jerk he really is. They must have no idea the kinds of secrets he keeps locked away. If they knew the things I know, they'd stay far, far away from him.

One of them tugs at his sleeve and says something, and he glances out toward the floor. Did she just ask him to dance?

They keep talking for a minute, and I have a perfect view of his profile. Of his dark hair and bright brooding eyes, of his full lips and strong jaw, of his broad shoulders and that ridiculous neckcloth he has tied in a thousand knots around his throat. He walks away from the girl, but he looks more like he's strutting.

I snicker to myself. He looks like a cat on the prowl, or maybe a peacock. Actually, a peacock isn't a bad analogy, considering how conceited and proud he is.

And that's when the song transitions and the crowd dissipates as new dancers swarm the floor. Before I can say a word, Emily hands me her glass and dashes off to find her . . . boyfriend? I guess he's just her crush. They probably don't even *have* boyfriends in this century.

I stand on the edge of the floor, suddenly filled with déjà vu. Why is this like every dance I've ever been to? Not that I have a long history or anything. I went to the 8th grade graduation dance though. And I did *try* to go to homecoming stag with Katie, but we only stayed twenty minutes. It turned out she was wrong about a lot of people going without dates, and we stood out like a couple of losers. We'd gone home and rented movies and pretended we hadn't wanted to be there anyway.

I glance around, hyperaware of every movement, knowing I look like a total dork. There are some chairs near the edge of the room, practically disappearing into some velvet curtains, so I scurry to them. Once sitting, I lean back. I'm not quite covered but I feel a little less obtrusive, like maybe no one will even notice I'm here.

I play with the fingers on my gloves and try to pretend I'm not being a complete wallflower.

I take a deep, calming breath. *This is 1815. I am Rebecca. And everyone loves Rebecca, with her fun piano duets and her tales of America.*

From my vantage point I've got a pretty good view of the scene. I can figure out a strategy for the next dance if I watch carefully. A woman seems to be in charge and is deciding exactly how the dance will work. Then the next person imitates her steps. Maybe she is Mrs. Pommeroy. Or Lady Pommeroy. Whatever. I study the dance for ten full minutes, trying to memorize what they're doing. It's actually pretty repetitive. A twirl here, a patty-cake there, and then down the line they go. I can probably pull it off. If someone asks me to dance, that is.

It just goes on and on and on. Fifteen minutes and they're still going. I find Emily in the sea of faces, and she's beaming from ear-to-ear. Trent is staring back at her as if she's the only girl in the room.

Yes, they are in love, even if they don't know it yet. I watch them for the next five minutes. Now and then wax drips from the chandeliers above, but they never take their eyes off of each other. They just laugh and dance and stare, and I bet the house could catch fire and they wouldn't even notice.

Emily is my friend, but watching her with that happy glow, I feel a familiar twinge. I've never had that. Not in the twenty-first century, not ever. Even Katie got a boyfriend a month after she moved away. But here I am, fifteen, never been kissed. Why? What's wrong with me? Am I that unworthy?

I stand up again, awkwardly because of the stiff corset, and nearly run into a girl maybe two years older than me. She has golden hair the color of straw, but it's twisted up in several plaits, so it makes her look over-Botoxed and angry.

"Oh, I'm, uh, I'm sorry. Excuse me."

But when I turn around, Alex is standing in front of me, an older guy trailing behind him. I've landed myself in the midst of two strangers and a guy I *wish* was a stranger. I so should have stayed hidden in the curtains.

"I see you've met Lady Everson," Alex says, gesturing to the blonde I'd crashed into. "Lady Everson, this is Miss Rebecca Vaughn, a guest at Harksbury."

I furrow my brow. "Why is she a lady and I'm a *miss*?"

His lips part. I've caught him totally off-guard. "Excuse me?"

"Why didn't you call *me* a lady?"

The girl stifles a giggle and steps closer, like she's about to watch a verbal smackdown and needs a better view. The stranger behind Alex also crowds closer. We have an audience, it seems.

"Because you are not a lady."

My jaw drops. "What's that supposed to mean?"

He quirks a brow and looks at me like I'm asking a stupid question. "A lady is a member of the peerage. Through marriage or lineage. You are neither."

Oh, this is rich, coming from a guy with an illegitimate kid.

"Where I come from, you're a lady because you act like one. Because you carry yourself with dignity and respect. You're not handed the title because of some fancy pedigree."

He arches a brow but says nothing.

Harrumph! The nerve! To say I'm not a lady! To introduce me to this girl as if she's better than me! When will he get over his elitist attitude and realize I'm just as good as everyone else even if I *am* a commoner?

The stranger clears his throat. "Excuse me, Your Grace," he says, bowing.

Alex bows back, though not as deeply. I wonder if that means the guy is of a lower rank. The idea is amusing, as Alex looks a great deal younger than him.

"Evening, Lord Brimmon," Alex says. His voice is cool and detached, just like last night at the dinner table.

"A nice evening for a dance, yes?" The guy is at least in his twenties, with a reddish tint to his brown hair. It's shorter than Alex's and a little bit unruly, but he has sparkling hazel eyes and a lean build, so he's still fairly cute. For, you know, an older guy.

"I suppose," Alex replies. His eyes flicker over to me and the girl. Does he think I'm going to start a cat fight when he's not looking? Please. *He's* the one I can't stand. I have nothing against this girl.

"Might you introduce me to these two lovely ladies?"

I smirk. The guy just called me a lady. I guess *he* was giving me the benefit of the doubt.

"Certainly. Might I introduce you to Lady Everson and Miss Rebecca Vaughn."

It's hard not to scowl at his continued snub.

"So lovely to meet you, Lady Everson, Miss Vaughn. Do you suppose you might like to dance?"

When I come up from my curtsy, I realize he's looking at *me*. I think I stop breathing for a second, because every muscle in my body freezes. I don't even blink. This guy wants to dance with me instead of this "lady." It's exactly what I wanted, and yet I'm paralyzed with terror. I don't know how. I've never even been asked to dance. Ever. Equal parts of anxiety and elation race through me.

"Wouldn't you prefer to dance with Lady Everson?" Alex says. And then before I know what he's doing, he's gently pushing Lady Everson forward and stepping in front of me, blocking my view of Brimmon. "She is a peer, after all."

I'm so stunned; the two disappear before I can even move.

When Alex turns to me, I come unleashed. "You are the rudest, most ridiculously arrogant person I have ever met in my life!" I say, and then spin on my heel and stomp away.

I've gone less than two yards before he stops me, a hand on my shoulder. "Miss Vaughn. As you are my guest, it is expected that the two of us shall dance."

I snort. "Oh, no, that's not necessary. I won't be your charity case. Wouldn't you rather—"

But he grabs my hand, places it on his elbow, and starts pulling me toward the floor just as the music transitions. Half the guests are looking at us. I can hardly rip my arm away and stomp on his foot without looking like a total freak. Not if I want a *nice* guy to ask me to dance later.

Besides, if Emily's right, I can't decline the first guy to ask me, or it will signal that I don't want to dance all night.

I hadn't imagined the first guy would be Alex.

Argh.

We take our places in the middle of the line up. He bows, and so I curtsy, and then follow his lead as we walk forward and back a few times, standing on our toes when we're close, and bowing down a bit as we step away. Everything I do is a half step behind him, but we're managing.

My anger still simmers below the surface. This is preposterous. He'll dance with me because he has to, but he thinks I'm not actually good enough for him—or for anyone with a title. I knew my first impression of him would prove correct. I knew he wasn't worth the ground I spit on! Talk about insulting!

He holds his hand up, palms facing me, so I push my hand against his and we sort of walk in a circle, our gloved hands palm to palm. Thank God we're wearing gloves; I don't want to touch this jerk.

We swap and circle the opposite way, our right hands touching this time.

The dance seems to be only a slight variation of the one I'd watched Emily do for the last half hour, and I manage to catch on by the third repetition. I actually feel kind of ridiculous because once we bow and spin and do-si-do, there's this part where we clap our hands together. And I haven't patty-caked for, like, ten years at least. But you know what they say—*when in Rome*. And I guess I am wearing a corset and all that, so I might as well go all the way. I'm just lucky I haven't tripped on my dress. It brushes the floor all around me, it's so long.

Does he seriously think I'm not good enough for Lord Brimmon? I might not be titled like half these people, but jeez, the guy's not asking me to marry him, he just wants to dance. I can't taint his reputation *that* quickly.

After about ten minutes I actually forget where I am—and who I'm dancing with—and start having fun. Alex and I manage to make our way to the end of the row of people, which is our cue to do this silly parade back to the end, where his arm is linked in mine and we kind of skip along. I'm actually smiling. I think it might be the first time since I arrived in this crazy world that I'm not worried about getting home or focused on the ridiculous, unbelievable nature of my predicament. I'm actually relaxed and having fun without stressing about what other people think of me. Truthfully, it's hard to remember feeling this unselfconscious in my own, real, twenty-first-century world. It feels nice. And free. I want it to last forever.

The dance is set up to impede conversation, so it's actually pretty easy to forget I'm dancing with Alex.

I'm breathing a little hard. My barely existent boobs are pushed up practically to my chin and my ribcage isn't exactly expanding, thanks to the corset, so it's a little hard to catch my breath.

When he breaks our silence, he's hesitant. "I did not mean to . . . insult you . . . earlier."

"*Right*," I say, in a way that makes it obvious I'm not buying it.

"Truly. I hadn't meant—"

"To treat me like I'm second class?" I don't want to have this conversation. I don't want to have *any* conversation.

We spin around and then part, and he has no chance to reply. I loop around another couple and then return to him. "Never mind. I don't need an answer. It's, you know, okay. Really. I'm, uh, it's fine." I'm rambling again and I sound bitter. Or offended. Which is the last thing I want because then he'll know his words actually *bothered* me, when I so don't care what he thinks of me.

"You think me pretentious," he says, when we come together again. It's spoken as a statement, not a question.

I look up at him, trying to see if he's angry. But no, he's just staring back, waiting for an answer. His face is neutral, but his brows are knotted slightly in concern, which makes it even harder to figure out what I'm supposed to say. Should I be honest?

"Of course. I have no idea why you'd want to dance with me. *You could hardly dance with a woman of my standing*," I say, my voice dripping with sarcasm. Too late, I realize I've said too much. I might hate him, but I can't be all-out rude to the guy I have to ride home with. The guy whose house I'm living in. "You know what? Never mind. Let's just dance. In silence," I say.

A moment later, the song is over, and I drop his hand.

He bows to me, and I curtsy, but I'm not looking at him.

He might be hot, but he's an even bigger jerk than I'd imagined.

18

The next day, Emily is doing her best to show me one of her finer skills: needlepoint.

I suck at it. It took me ten minutes just to get the needle threaded, and then it promptly fell off.

I'm pretty sure this means I'd make a terrible wife in the 1800s. Needlepoint is like the ABCs of wifery or something. Emily, on the other hand, is taking it quite seriously, sitting regally on a brocade chair, her needle darting in and out of the fabric at a lightning pace.

We're in some kind of sitting room or drawing room or whatever it's called (they have too many rooms, if you ask me) on the first floor, in the west wing. This one is a vibrant sea of blue, from the curtains to the carpet, and the painting over the elaborate hearth is of a ship being tossed around in a storm. It was sort of jarring, to walk into this room and be assaulted by blue.

I'm sucking on the end of the thread, trying to get it to

straighten out, when Alex strides in.

He bows to the two of us, and when he speaks, his voice fills the room, far louder and more booming than a voice should be before noon. "I intend to ride the estate today, if you two would like to join me."

I open my mouth to give him a quick, *No thanks, I'd rather pull out my own hair,* but Emily beats me to it.

"How kind of you to offer! We would love to."

Huh? I can't figure out why Emily doesn't hate Alex. He's a jerk and he's done nothing to help her out of her engagement. And now she's volunteering to hang out with him?

An excuse . . . I need some kind of excuse to get out of this.

Alex walks to the window and looks out, offering a rather flattering view of the back of his riding pants. "Did you enjoy the dance last evening?"

Is he making small talk? That's a first. "Yes, very much so," Emily says. "It was delightful."

I nod. "Yeah. I guess so." I won't say I had fun because I don't want him to get the wrong idea. I don't want him to know dancing with him was the most exciting part of my evening *and* the most agonizingly long half hour of my life.

Alex looks at me for a long silent moment. You'd think he'd bring up the big "lady" versus "miss" debacle. Or just that we'd danced. But he doesn't.

"Yes, I rather enjoyed myself as well," he says.

Seriously, what does that mean? I was the only girl he danced with. The entire night. Is he trying to tell me something? Ha.

Right. He probably means that it was all sorts of fun to insult me.

And that's when Emily starts rubbing her temple. She sets her needlepoint down and frowns, massaging in circular motions on the side of her face.

Oh, no, she's not—

"Dear cousin, I am coming down with a headache. Perhaps you and Rebecca ought to ride without me."

I get a twinge when I hear *Rebecca*. Every day it feels more like we're friends—and more like I'm betraying her.

And then she turns to me, knowing Alex can't see her, and *winks*.

"Oh, no, I—" I start to say, because I suddenly realize what she's trying to do. This *can not* happen. A horseback ride alone with Alex? No thank you!

But Alex cuts in before I can stop her. "Yes, I would not have you overexerting yourself. We shall check on you when we return."

Okay, this is not how I want to spend my afternoon. Alone with Alex? I'd rather get a root canal.

But . . . maybe it's my chance to talk to him about Emily. Maybe he doesn't know about Trent. Emily said Trent was wealthy, right? He's not titled, but he has money. If Alex knew about him . . . maybe he would get Emily off the hook with Denworth.

Maybe *that's* why Emily is trying to arrange for me to spend time with Alex. She so owes me after this.

I can do this. I can hang out with him for a couple hours—

long enough to talk him into helping us.

Emily jumps up from her chair far too quickly for someone with a headach and leaves the room before I can do anything.

I rub my eyes. It's going to be a long afternoon.

19

"Okay, so I take my foot," I say, pointing to the toe of my Prada heel, "and stick it in that . . . *thing?*"

This whole trip is turning into a nightmare. First I had to change into a *riding habit*, as if I have any idea what that is. And now I'm supposed to ride *sidesaddle.* Seriously. Isn't riding with one foot on each side of the horse hard enough already? I can't even drive a car yet!

Alex nods. "The stirrup." He has one hand on the horse's reins and the other holding the stirrup out for me. Two grooms are hovering in the background, looking a little put out. I think they had planned to help me up. Alex is standing so close I can smell him, this masculine musky scent that makes me want to rest my head on his chest and breathe in.

Which is absurd, and I need to stop thinking about it.

Wretched human being. Remember that.

I jam my foot in the stirrup and have to sort of hip-hop around a few times to keep from falling down, and then my foot slips out and I'm just standing there again. The horse swings its head around and looks at me as if to say *you're* still *standing there?*

Alex doesn't say anything, just stands stock-still, holding the horse and waiting for me to get my act together. He's probably groaning inwardly at my incompetence.

I try again. This time manage to get my foot into the stirrup and my hands toward the seat of the saddle, and, after taking a few hops, stand up and put my weight into the stirrup. Alex has to grab my waist and boost me up in order to get me all the way to the seat, and then I almost fall off the other side as I figure out how to hook my knee onto the saddle. It takes almost five minutes for me to get situated as he continues to stand there, holding the reins so the horse won't move until I'm ready. "Thanks," I say.

I can feel the spot where his fingers touched my hips like they're still there, holding me. Not cool.

"Certainly," he says as he releases the reins. "Are you ready?"

I nod and the reins are suddenly out of his grasp and I tighten them so hard the horse starts to back up. "Oh, uh . . . What do I do?!" I panic because the horse is, well, *moving*. In the wrong direction.

Alex comes back over to me. "Release your hold. I promise you this horse will not run away with you. Keep some slack in the reins. Too tight and she'll think you want her to back up. She's only trying to please you." His voice is calm and cool.

I nod and relax my hand just a bit, until the reins have a

bit of a droop in them. I resist the urge to immediately snatch them back up. "Trust me," he says, looking straight at me.

And as I stare back at him, I just nod dumbly, suddenly believing I trust him. Which is the *wrong* thing to feel. I'm willing to bet Mystery Mistress trusted him too, and look how well that turned out!

I mean, come on. This is a guy who is screwing over his own cousin, who insulted me at the dance and abandoned his own kid. I can *not* trust him.

He walks back over to his gray stallion and swings up easily, even though it's probably a foot taller than the one I'm on. He looks perfect in his boots and jacket, like something out of a catalog. Even though I've never seen clothes like that in a catalog. God, what am I thinking?

We pick up a walk. I'm gripping onto the little copper horse's reins like my life depends on it. Alex looks very much at ease, even as the horse dances excitedly underneath him, its legs flexing and skipping around at twice the speed they need to. Just watching it makes me nervous.

Is he going to apologize, or what? He knows I was bothered by what he said at the dance. He has to say something, right? If he thinks he can just forget about it, he's wrong.

"I do hope Emily is well," he says, as we pass the barns and head up a grassy knoll.

"Oh, I'm sure she's fine," I say dryly. "In fact, I'm certain she'll feel totally healthy by the time we return."

Healthy enough to bombard me and ask how this whole ride went.

The weather is beautiful today: blue skies and a warm breeze. In fact, given the three layers I must be wearing, it's a tad on the warm side. There seem to be birds everywhere, from the tree limbs and fence rails around us to the sky above us, chirping and squawking. Everything smells so *fresh*. And clean, and just . . . new.

"Do you own all this?" We've crested the small hill and fields and fields stretch out before me, trees dotting the landscape, with a forest up ahead. The place is bigger than my entire neighborhood back home. Bigger than the school and the stadium and the baseball fields.

"Yes. Twelve thousand acres."

"You mean twelve hundred."

He laughs. It's short and quiet, but it's a *laugh*, and I can't believe I actually heard it. "No. Twelve thousand."

I swallow. Twelve thousand acres. A square mile is six hundred forty. Yes, just knowing that makes me a nerd. So his property is—I do the math in my head—over eighteen and three-quarters square miles. No wonder we're twelve miles from town. No wonder there were no other rooftops for so long. No wonder we had to go so far to get to the Pommeroy estate.

Because Alex owns half the land between here and there.

"I see." I try to suppress my awe. "And what do you . . . do with all that? Farm?"

He shakes his head. "No, I manage the tenant farmers. They live on the other side of the trees. I use the land between for fox hunting."

Ew. Fox hunting. Yet another of his delightful qualities. "That's cruel."

He looks over at me, one eyebrow lifted. "How so?"

"We learned about it in . . . a book." Way to go, I actually manage to stop myself from saying history class. "You block off all the fox dens so that the foxes can't get back home. And then you release dogs and let them tear the foxes to bits when they find one."

He nods, his lips pursed together. I try not to stare at them.

"And exactly how does that prove *your* skill? All you do is ride around at breakneck speed to keep up with the dogs. You don't actually hunt the fox using your own skill—it's the dogs'. Why not just race around on your horse instead of killing some poor animal?"

"Women never understand the appeal of the hunt."

I snort. "There you go again, acting like we're a lesser species."

"It is men who have conquered this world," he states matter-of-factly.

"You're hopeless," I say, more disgusted than ever.

We ride into the woods, and the shade feels much cooler. I hope it keeps my face from flushing. I'm sweating underneath all these layers. We follow a wide path winding between dozens of oak trees, their limbs twisting toward the sky.

"The air always seems fresher in the woods," he says in an obvious attempt to avoid arguing.

"It is. Fresher, I mean. Plants breathe in carbon dioxide and release oxygen."

Alex twists around to stare straight at me. "You're simply full of scientific knowledge, aren't you?"

And he says it in the most annoying, condescending manner. I want to strangle him.

"God, you really hate that I know things you don't."

He scowls and turns forward again. "Of course not."

"Whatever. You're not used to being one-upped by a girl. Admit it."

"I'll do no such thing."

"Okay then, how about we talk science? Bet you didn't know that you blink more than four million times per year."

His expression remains unchanged, though I'm almost positive he's trying not to blink.

"And did you know it takes fourteen inches of snow to equal one inch of rain?"

His eyes are narrowed, but he hasn't spoken yet.

"Or how about that you lose most of your body heat through your head?"

"You've proven your point," he says.

"And yet I bet you haven't changed your mind about me," I say. "You're far too stubborn for that."

The conversation dies away when he moves in front of me on the trail, and we continue our ride in silence. I have a good view of him from here, and I can watch him without him knowing. And I like the way he looks relaxed. He's more at ease on a thousand-pound horse than at the dinner table. Oh sure, his shoulders are still squared, and his back is still straight, but he's sort of swaying with the horse's bouncy peppy gait, his hands giving and taking on the reins like they're rubber bands.

"Easy, Ghost," Alex says as we descend a small hill toward a creek. I can see his horse is nervous because its hindquarters swing sideways until the horse is actually walking that way, crossing its legs over one another as Alex pushes it toward the shallow water. "Give me a bit of room, in case Ghost gets any ideas."

I nod and pull lightly on the reins, trying not to overdo it like when I'd gotten on. The little mare eases to a stop and I try to relax my grip. I take the opportunity to rearrange the skirts of my gown, trying to get them to cover my feet.

Ghost is dancing around in the mud now, not wanting anything to do with the creek in front of us. His hooves are picking up, two at a time, making funny sucking noises in the slop. Alex is leaning the slightest bit forward, his hands resting on the horse's neck, like he's not at all worried about hanging on if the horse takes off. How can he look so comfortable? The thing looks like it's ready to bolt.

The horse takes a couple funny bouncy steps and then lifts both front hooves and takes a flying leap over the water. Alex never leaves the saddle. He never looks fazed.

In fact, when he lands on the other side, he laughs—a real, no-mistaking-it laugh—and the sound is music to my ears. I wish he'd do it a thousand more times. Until this moment, I thought he didn't even *have* a real laugh.

Oh God, I should not be charmed by a simple laugh.

Jerk. Jerk. Jerk. I can't forget that.

He pats the horse's neck. "That's not quite what I had in mind." And then he turns around and tries again. The horse jumps again and ends up splashing in the creek. Alex is beaming. He turns around and crosses three more times, and by the end, the horse is plodding through like he's been doing it all day.

"We can go now."

I don't release the reins. "This horse isn't going to do that, is she?"

He shakes his head, and then he smiles at me. Directly at me. All the dislike I'd felt melts away in an instant, and I want to stand here all day in the glow of his smile. His lips are curled, and his eyes are sparkling in a way I couldn't have imagined. And I suddenly want to be close to him. Really, really close to him.

You are not a lady. I remember his words and bite back the urge to smile. *Is it so easy to forget your whispered promises?*

There are so many reasons I should stay far, far away from him. There's no way I'm going to forget about all that just because he smiles at me. Even if it is a totally devastating smile.

"No. Molly is an old hack of mine. She has been everywhere. She will cross without even looking at the water first."

I nod and click my tongue, too afraid to actually nudge the horse's sides in case she gets any funny ideas. But true to Alex's word, the horse plods down the bank, crosses the creek with a few splashy steps, and then I'm next to Alex again.

"Thank you for your patience," he says. "Ghost is still quite green. Though I am certain you noticed."

I just nod because I can't figure out why he's acting so happy. So nice. So . . . not like him. Ten minutes ago he was acting like there was no way I was smarter than him. How can he be *this* Alex and the other one too?

I try to make small talk. "So, what does it mean to be a duke, really?"

He straightens even more in his saddle, proving his shoulders apparently *can* go further back. All I have to do is mention the fact that he's a duke, and suddenly he's a peacock again. "The Dukedom of Harksbury was created by the king in return for years of service and loyalty from my great-great-great-grandfather. As the firstborn son, I inherited the title, the land, and the wealth. Each year I will serve our great country in the House of Lords, helping to create new laws. And then in the summer I return to Harksbury and see to the household matters. It is my duty to see that all here prosper."

All *here* prosper? What about all *there*? As in far, far away, with a baby? How can he act like he's this great, magnanimous guy and ignore those letters?

One thing at a time. I need to bring up Emily's engagement somehow. There's got to be a good opening if I keep him talking.

"So . . . all these other lords. Are you guys all equal or is there some kind of ranking system?" I hope this is all normal stuff to ask. Even though they don't have peers in America, someone in 1815 would probably still know what they were. But he doesn't know that, right?

"A duke is the highest member of the peerage. Under the royal family, of course. The older the title, the more prestigious. Under a duke is a marquess, followed by earl, viscount, and baron."

Okay, I have to stop stalling. I have to talk to him about Emily and Trent. "So, you have a lot of power then, right?"

That's it. I'll stroke his gigantic ego first and then segue into a plea for help.

He nods. "Yes, power comes with being a member of the peerage."

"Don't you ever want to use that power to help people?"

"Certainly."

Here goes nothing.

"The thing is, I met this guy named Trent Rallsmouth last night. He and Emily . . . like each other. A lot. And she says he's wealthy."

"And?"

"And so I think they should get married instead of her and Lord Denworth."

"I thought we'd agreed you would stop this and mind your place."

"I'll stop when Emily gets to marry the guy she wants to marry."

"Emily will marry Denworth because that is what she was told to do. She can not choose otherwise because of a passing fancy for another man."

"But—"

"*No.*"

Okay. I can forget about Alex helping us. Conversation over.

I can't believe I thought he'd help. At all. He definitely does not care about Emily, or anyone else for that matter.

He cares about himself. And that's it.

But I'm not giving up. I promised Emily. There has to be something I can do. I'm from the twenty-first century. Land of equal opportunity and all that crap. I know things these people don't even know to dream of. I have to come up with something.

But what can I do? All I know is Emily's the only reason I'm not starving to death somewhere in the woods. If she hadn't been at the door that day, I would have been turned away.

And now, thanks to my lies, she believes I'm going to help her. If I want to channel my inner-Rebecca, if I want to be confident and casual and popular, I have to live up to her expectations. I have to fix this. Besides, if it's truly why I ended up here, then helping Emily *must* lead me to the way home.

If Alex won't help me, I'll figure it out myself.

I have to. If I don't, I might be stuck here.

Forever.

20

The next morning, I'm sitting in the sunny little breakfast room, willing Victoria to stop shoveling eggs in her mouth so I can talk to Emily.

Emily and I need to come up with a plan as soon as possible. I have no idea when her wedding is . . . but didn't they love shotgun weddings or something back in the day?

Plus, the real Rebecca's arrival is creeping closer. Less than three weeks, now. Every day gets me closer to discovery.

Heck, what if the real Rebecca arrives early? She could randomly show up *today* for all I know. What if I'm sitting with them all over some random meal and Rebecca strolls in? What do they do to people who scam their way into the household? I definitely don't want to find out. Alex doesn't strike me as the forgiving type.

"Did the two of you enjoy the dance at the Pommeroy estate?"

Great. So Victoria is done eating but she's not leaving.

Instead she's sitting up in her chair with posture fit for a queen, staring at the two of us like bugs under a microscope. I'm not sure what it is about her that bothers me so much. She's more intimidating than Angela and Trisha Marks combined.

"Yes, quite," Emily says.

"Lady Tonoway tells me you danced with His Grace," she says. She's staring straight at me with those piercing green eyes, like laser beams that will cut me to ribbons if I answer the wrong way.

I can't seem to ignore the sinking feeling low in my stomach. This can't be good. Not with a glare like that.

"Yes," I say, after a moment's hesitation.

"That was . . . *polite* of him."

Polite of him. Like he'd done it out of duty. Which, honestly, he said as much himself. I clench my jaw, hard.

I know he did it out of duty, since I'm his guest. But she doesn't know that—she doesn't know what he said before we danced. She's just trying to be condescending.

And as much as I hate it, I know what she's saying is true. Alex hates me as much as I hate him, so it makes sense. He was doing his gentlemanly duty.

But it still makes me want to snap at her.

I will not blurt out something stupid.

I will not blurt out something stupid.

"Yes. He's quite . . . *polite*, isn't he? He must be, since he doesn't like dancing. I was the only girl he danced with." I smile right at her, stick a piece of meat in my mouth, and chew it with gusto.

Emily's fork stops moving, she looks up at me, and I see her swallow slowly. She wills me with her eyes to stop talking. "Shall we go for a turn about the garden, Rebecca?"

There it is again. Rebecca. I try to smile at her, but my lips barely move.

Emily and I are away from the table so quickly I'm not sure Victoria has even thought of a reply to my statement, and I enjoy the lost look on her face as we dash out of the room.

"I should think Victoria will be stewing over this for hours." Emily doesn't sound angry or even surprised, but rather amused. There's a devilish smirk I hardly recognize playing at the edges of her lips. "You shall have to teach me how to do that."

"Do what?"

We're out the door now and into the sun, and she links her arm with mine. Our skirts brush now and then as we walk along a cobbled path. "Send her off-kilter when she's trying so hard to have the upper hand."

"It's not so much a talent as an impulse. I'm afraid I have no restraint. You, on the other hand, manage to take things in stride and be graceful about it."

Emily smiles. "Perhaps if I knew how to speak as directly as you do, I could convince my father to break my engagement to a man I have no interest in knowing."

I have to fight the urge to laugh. In real life I'm the last person to stick up for myself—or for anyone else. I'm tongue-tied and shy. And yet . . . I feel a little empowered by the fact that Emily thinks of me differently. Like I can prove her right and prove everyone else wrong.

I stop next to a rosebush and, as they say, *smell the roses.*
I linger over a small yellow bud. It buys me time to think of
what to say next. "Do you think he would listen? Perhaps I
can speak with him. Make him understand."

If she thinks that might work, the solution is simple.

Plan A: Talk to Emily's father.

She sighs and fiddles with the folds of her skirt. "Not at all.
What my father wants, my father gets. There's no hope of
swaying him."

I sigh and turn back toward her. Darn. So much for Plan A.

She plops down on a stone bench and buries her face in
her hands.

I can't let her give up that easily. There's got to be a way
out of an arranged marriage. It probably happens all the time,
right?

"What about if we find some really great girl who *wants* to
marry Denworth? Like maybe he's got a thing for blondes or
redheads or really tall girls. We can do some legwork and find
out what kind of girl he's into. If we find someone perfect,
he'll forget all about you."

Plan B: Bait and Switch.

She shakes her head. "No, that would never do. Denworth's
word is good. He'll never break it."

Hm. Nix Plan B.

"Oh." I twist the little yellow bud in my hand until it snaps
off and I'm left with it in my palm, my thumb smoothing over
the petals. "Well, there have to be *some* broken engagements
in the history of this country, right?"

Emily nods but I still can't see her face. I hope she's not crying. I don't want to make her think it's *more* hopeless.

"What kinds of things do people do to initiate that?" I peel the petals off the bud one at a time and let them flutter to the ground. I hope she doesn't remind me that I told her I had tons of ideas.

She looks up, and I'm relieved to see that her eyes aren't shiny. She taps her chin and screws her mouth to the side, deep in thought. "Most often out of mutual agreement, though that would never happen with Denworth. Sometimes after scandals are uncovered, like a bankruptcy, or if someone was discovered to be illegitimate."

I cringe, the word *illegitimate* bringing up images of that letter to Alex.

She sighs. "Other times . . . Well, if the woman were discovered to be . . . " Emily looks around and then speaks in a low, hushed tone, *"ruined,* that would certainly be cause for a broken engagement. Why, Lord Forsythe broke an engagement to the daughter of the Earl of Bowmont just last season. It was quite the scandal."

I perk up. "What do you mean, ruined?"

From the way Emily swallows slowly, you'd think we were talking about smoking crack. I think I've scandalized her *already.* "Compromised. By . . . by another man."

"Oh!" I say, too loudly. "You mean, if the girl's not a virgin, the guy won't marry her?"

She nods, her eyes wide, as if being a non-virgin is akin to being an ax-murderer.

"Well, let's do that!"

Emily looks so shocked I think I could nudge her shoulder and she'd fall right over and into the rose bushes.

"I don't mean, *actually* do it . . . But can't we fake it?"

She's a little pale as she shakes her head, and it makes me laugh.

"I think you're misinterpreting me. What I mean is . . . can't we just make it *look* like you're, uh, compromised? You don't actually have to do anything. But if we can get people to believe it, maybe spread some rumors, Denworth will drop you like a hot potato. Problem solved."

Emily is shaking her head like I'm crazy. "You mean to stage a ruination?"

I bite back a laugh because the way she's saying it makes it seem wild and crazy and yet somehow like it's a formal process. "It could work, right? I mean, if your rep is tarnished, Denworth wouldn't want to marry you?"

She nods. "But everyone would believe I was immoral!"

"Immoral? Really?" I pause. I can see Emily isn't going to go along with this very easily. "But it could work. And in a year or two, no one would remember the scandal at all, and you'd live happily ever after with Trent."

"I can't possibly."

"You'd rather marry Denworth?"

My question hangs in the air as Emily plays with the folds of her skirt, staring down at the sheer fabric as if it's a Magic 8 Ball.

"How would it work?"

"We would come up with a plan for people to think you'd been alone with Trent. That's against the rules, right? You guys are supposed to have chaperones if you're together?" I snap another rosebud off the nearest bush, full of nervous energy. This could work, if she'll agree to it. I could fix the engagement and get her together with Trent.

She nods.

"So we'd tell everyone you spent the night alone with him. That would be enough. But if everyone thinks you're ruined, that's got to mean that everyone, not just Denworth, would stay away from you, right? If you're not good enough for Denworth, that would be the general consensus of society."

Emily furrows her brow and nods, looking like she's going to pitch her breakfast at any moment. Her gorgeous pale skin has gone ash-white.

"But if we could get Mr. Rallsmouth to agree in advance, make sure he wants to marry you even with the ruined reputation, it could work."

She nods again, slowly, like she doesn't want to follow my line of reasoning.

"It's our only choice. We have to do it. Let's talk to him and put the plan in motion. Let's get you engaged to Mr. Rallsmouth."

Plan C: Ruin Emily.

21

Only two hours pass before I start wondering if putting all our eggs in one basket is such a hot idea. What if we get it all set up and then Trent backs out? Then everyone will think she's not a virgin, and *no one* will marry her.

There are some serious flaws in this plan. But I'm afraid to bring them up, because Emily is just barely going along with it. I think she might have a heart attack or spontaneously combust at any moment.

God, this is stupid. There has to be a plan that's less risky than this one.

I sent Trent a note about an hour ago, explaining the whole thing. If he agrees, he'll arrive tonight and sweep Emily away for an evening. I can't back out now, no matter how panicked I feel.

It will work. What could possibly go wrong? If Trent agrees, he's going to marry her. Problem solved.

Alex must be dealing with some of his dukely duties or

something, because he's gone for the day. It's perfect, though, because Emily and I need a day to talk and scheme and not worry about him figuring out what we're plotting.

We're really going to try to do this. I'm both thrilled and terrified because I want it to work so badly. If it doesn't . . . What then? I'll have gotten her hopes up for nothing. And probably made things worse. And I can't take the idea of disappointing her.

I hope I've thought of everything.

I help Emily pack a trunk's worth of clothes while we wait for a response from Trent. We're trying to keep as many people in the dark about this as possible, which means no more servants than necessary. "Below stairs," as it really is called, is a rumor mill. Worse than high school. Not that I blame them. It's sort of like the way the majority of the high school talks about the A-list.

Of course, when it's time, the servants will become part of our plan. They'll play their role: push the rumor that Emily is ruined. But if they know too early, they'll tip off Victoria or Alex, who will stop us before we start.

"This is so very thrilling!" Emily says, stuffing another gown into the trunk. "Everyone will be so shocked when they discover I'm gone." She's buzzing with energy; she can hardly sit still. Her cheeks are flushed and her eyes are sparkling as she dances around the room and picks out more gowns.

"I'll cover for you until we're ready for Phase 2," I say, even though I don't have a clue how I'm going to do it. "They won't even know you're gone until I'm ready for them to know."

Why do I keep telling her this stuff? I have no idea how to cover for her. Normally, I could just tell everyone she's not feeling well . . . But wouldn't a servant wait on her? They're going to think it's weird if *I* offer to bring her food.

Oh, well. I'm sure something brilliant will come to me.

There's a knock on the door and both of us stare at each other, wide-eyed as we flip the trunk shut and find seats, trying to act as if we're up to nothing at all. It couldn't be more obvious if we whistled nonchalantly.

"You may enter," Emily calls out in a voice much calmer than I feel.

A servant walks in and hands her a note before curtsying and leaving.

Emily holds it in one shaky hand and stares at the scrawled name on the outside.

"Open it!"

She just keeps staring.

"Oh fine, let me open it!"

She holds the note out to me. I snatch it from her hand and then slide a thumb under the edge to pop open the wax seal. My eyes scan over the first few words before a grin spreads across my features. "He's in! He's agreed to run away with you!"

Emily jumps up and nearly knocks me over with a hug. Her laughter tickles my ear, and before I know it we both fall over and end up rolling on the floor, laughing and squealing. The plan is falling into place. Just like I thought it would.

"I cannot believe he agreed! Oh, he has made me the happiest girl in all of England!"

I nod. I should feel relieved, but I just feel nervous. This has to work. It has to. It's my ticket home. I'm sure of it. What other way could there be?

Emily and I dust off our dresses and resume packing, shoving a few more items into the already-overflowing trunk. I'm not sure why she's packing so much when she only needs to be gone for a night, but it seems to be keeping her nerves at ease, so I don't stop her.

She pauses, her hand gripping a yellow slipper, and grins. "I knew you would help me. When I realized you'd arrived so early, I thought you were a gift from God. And now it seems I was right." She grins again as she resumes her packing, and I smile weakly at her. What if this falls apart? She's already writing her Academy Award thank you speech and nothing's fixed yet. If she knew my track record for screwing everything up . . .

I take a deep breath and grab the next pile of clothes. I have to stop thinking of it like that.

I've thought of everything. What could possibly go wrong?

After dinner, I wait on the cold front stoop for what seems like hours, watching the sky darken.

What if he doesn't come? What if his note was a lie and he doesn't show up? Maybe he chickened out. Maybe he realized this whole plan is totally nuts and he bailed on us. There are a thousand reasons he could back out.

I pace up and down between the big columns so many times I must be wearing a groove in the stone. There's a drizzle coming down. I'm dry, thanks to the overhang, but I keep watching and praying it doesn't turn into a full-blown storm and ruin everything. The sky darkens and the sun sets, and still he has not arrived.

Finally, just when I'm about to have a heart attack, I see a glow in the distance, bobbing along. It's getting brighter, and then a carriage emerges from the night shadows, a dark horse pulling it quietly along. When I see Trent atop the bench, cloaked in a dark jacket, sitting just under the canopy, I grin like a fool. It's a small carriage, built only for two: Trent and Emily. He pulls to a stop in front of the steps and starts to climb down.

"Wait here!" I say, in a shouted whisper. He can't be seen by *anyone* if Emily is to make a clean getaway. Trent just nods and sits back down. He doesn't even give me a weird look, which I have to give him credit for. Plan C: Phase 1 is complete. Time for Phase 2: Send Emily Away.

I turn and push the door open, and nearly run smack into the butler.

Oh, crud. I forgot about him. I shove the door closed before he can see Trent or his carriage, my heart hammering against my rib cage. What am I supposed to do now? He might alert Victoria or say something to Trent . . . Emily has to get away unnoticed.

"Grommley," Emily calls from the foot of the stairs. "Will you see to it that Mrs. West prepares the four guest chambers at the end of the east wing? I may be expecting visitors."

Genius. Pure genius.

Grommley—the butler—bows and leaves the door, and I manage to breathe again.

"Thank you," I say.

"Yes. Now let me fetch my things."

I nod and watch her climb back up the stairs and disappear. I'm still standing there, alone, when I see him.

Alex. He's walking down the east wing, a floor below Emily. Cripes, she's probably directly above him, grabbing her things. Does everyone have to appear at exactly this moment? Can I catch a break please?

His strides are so long he's going to be in front of me, and in the middle of the foyer, in three seconds. He's supposed to be asleep! I haven't seen him in hours . . . What is he doing? He's about to ruin it all!

22

A quick glance upward and I see Emily emerge from her quarters, two servants behind her to carry the trunk. She waves and opens her mouth to speak, but I do first.

"Alex," I say, more loudly than necessary. "Uh, good evening," I add with a clumsy curtsy. He nods his head back at me and bows. When his head is down, I look up to see Emily snap her mouth shut and stop so quickly the servants almost bump into her. I go tense and wait for Alex to hear the commotion behind him and up one floor, but he doesn't. He's looking at me. So I force my eyes away from her. It's not too late. I can divert him somehow.

Uh, right. How, exactly?

I try to stare right at him as I see, from the corner of my eye, Emily back up and motion to the others. They retreat into a nearby room, the door clicking shut behind them. The sound echoes into the foyer, much louder than I'd expected.

Alex steps forward and looks up when he hears the noise.

"Um, so, what's going on?" I say.

Turn around, I think. *Look at me.*

For a long second, his eyes remain on the door. What room is that? Are they not supposed to be in there or something? Did he see Emily up there? Does he know something's going on? He takes a step toward the stairs. What is he doing?

"Your letters," I blurt out.

God, why did I do that? It was the only thing I could think of. But I didn't want him to know that I knew about the kid. I wanted to read more of the letters and develop a plan.

I just hadn't done it yet. I got distracted by a dance and Emily's engagement. But now I have to give them back in order to help Emily get away.

"Pardon?" He turns to look at me again. Does he always have to look so hot? Those tall shiny boots, the stiff green jacket, the starched white necktie . . . I force my eyes shut and shake my head. I've been here too long if I think he looks *that* good.

"I, um, found some of your letters. In the library."

He tips his head a little and gives me a look I can't decipher.

My heart pounds harder. *Please* don't ask me what's going on. *Please* don't catch on. I step forward and smile. "If you'll come with me, I'll give them to you."

My room is in the hall opposite to where Emily is. If he follows me over there, Emily will be able to get away.

He purses his lips for a long moment, as I stare at him and try to figure out what's going on in his head, but then he just nods and I breathe a deep sigh of relief. "Very well," he says.

I gesture for him to follow me and we walk up the stairs, turning away from Emily in the east wing when we hit the landing, and heading toward the western one and my room.

We head down the hall. It seems to stretch forever. I think I hear Emily's door click open again but I cough to cover it, and Alex just gives me another odd look.

Whew. That was close.

Is he allowed to come into my room? I'm guessing not. God, I hope Emily is quiet. He can't see her from in front of my bedroom door, but he could definitely hear her if she created a ruckus.

"Hold on and I'll go get them, okay? Don't move a muscle," I say. Could I be more obvious? I'm really bad at this secret-agent stuff. It'll take at least a few more minutes for Emily to get her things loaded.

I dash into my room and head straight to the bed. The letters are jammed under the mattress. Bundle in hand, I head back to the open door. Alex is standing in the hallway, back several yards, as if just coming within arm's length of my room is a breach of etiquette. It almost makes me laugh. In fact, if it weren't for the bundle of letters practically burning a hole in my hand, I would.

I step back into the hall and am relieved when I hear only silence. I wonder if Emily is gone yet.

I grip the papers in my hands, not willing to let them go

when they could be full of secrets. If only I had taken the time to read them . . .

He steps forward to take them, but I can only grip them tighter in my hands. The thought of handing them over makes anger bubble up inside me.

If I succeed with Emily and she marries Trent, then I may end up back home.

And this little girl is going to be left behind, all alone. He's going to ignore her forever. I know it.

Jerk.

"How could you do that to her?" I ask.

"Excuse me? To whom?"

I snort and my lip curls up in disgust. The bubbling anger explodes. "Your daughter, you idiot! How could you just leave them like that? Do you even know if they're okay?"

He looks so shocked he physically recoils and steps back a few feet. "My *daughter?* I have no daughter, and it would do you well not to spread such vicious rumors."

I shake my head. "That's what you're afraid of, huh? You don't want people to know so you're ignoring her, hoping she goes away. But she won't. And I may have only read one of these letters, but I can tell how much it is hurting her that you're doing this."

The shock ebbs from his face and transforms into a look of dawning realization.

And then he laughs. It starts as a short burst and then rumbles into a full belly-shaking laugh. He puts a hand against a wall to support himself and holds one arm against his stomach. His huge figure curls over as he succumbs to the apparent hilarity he finds in the situation.

All I can do is stare at him. This is hardly the reaction I was expecting—nor was I expecting how truly adorable he looks when he's amused.

No. He is *not* adorable. "What is wrong with you?" I say, stepping closer. "Is this really a laughing matter?"

He gets his laughter under control and stands upright again, wiping a tear away from under his cheek.

"I simply find it extraordinary you think me of such loose morals that I could father a child and not do my duty to care for her."

"Then what is this?" I ask, shaking the letters.

"Did it not occur to you that they are addressed to my father?"

My jaw drops, and suddenly I'm frozen in place.

The Duke of Harskbury. *Your Grace.*

The name Alex appears nowhere on them. Had they been dated? Did I even look?

The baby is his *sister.*

"I—"

I'm at a total loss for words. All this time I'd watched him, steaming, believing he was having the time of his life living in this mansion and ignoring his responsibilities.

But it was his *father.*

I shove the letters toward him, hating the way they burn in my hands. "What happened to them?" I ask, my voice suddenly hoarse.

Alex sighs and stares at the bundle for a long silent moment, as if lost in another world. His eyes turn soft around the edges, contemplative.

"The child's name is Amelia. I had no clue of her existence until after my father had passed. I discovered the letters in his study. It took me three months to find them. By then Amelia was nearly three."

Alex twists his cufflinks, an idle fidget that seems more characteristic of me than of him. That cocky flair to his posture has vanished, and for the first time, he looks like a teenager. "The mother was working as a maid for a baronet. They were managing. But Amelia deserved better."

Does he look . . . *pained?* Cripes, the guy actually cares about her. How could I have been so far off?

"They live in one of my family homes up north. Greysbrooke, to be precise. With a full staff, including a governess for Amelia."

I swallow, hard, my heart beating in an unsettled, erratic rhythm. "You're taking care of them?"

He nods. "My father should not have left them to fend for themselves. She may be illegitimate, but she is a duke's daughter."

"I am sure they are doing marvelously now, thanks to you," I say, feeling like a complete and total jerk.

"It is my hope that I can avoid the worst of the scandal and Amelia may one day enter polite society. With me on her side, I can ensure she has everything she deserves."

I nod my head, a thousand words swimming in my mind,

but none surface. They're all lost somewhere inside.

I was wrong about him. And now here I am, sneaking around behind his back, thinking he deserves it all. Maybe I shouldn't be doing this right now. I'm basically lying to him right this instant to help Emily escape, and he doesn't even know it.

He spent months looking for a half sister he'd never known just to make sure she was okay. That's the kind of guy he is, apparently.

No, I refuse to believe that. He's been a jerk in all other aspects. Maybe he doesn't have a daughter, but he still thinks girls are second-rate. I shouldn't *have* to go behind his back; he should be helping Emily! But he's not, so I have to.

I refuse to feel guilty for this.

"Thank you for returning these," he says, bowing slightly. "I am not sure why I am compelled to keep them."

"Sure. No problem."

I can't think of anything else to say as he turns and walks away. I can only hope Emily is gone, or the plan is ruined.

I return to my room and walk to the window seat. The rain is coming down harder now, leaving rivulets of water on the windowpane. I can faintly make out the glow of a lantern beyond the glass, near the stables.

My own room is dark with shadows. A hot coal fire glows in the hearth, and a candle drips from its place on my little table. I sit on the window seat and pull my legs up beside me.

Emily is going to stay the night in a small gardener's cottage on the edge of Harksbury. She said no one has used it in at least two years, and no one will think of going there. She only has to be gone a single night for it to ruin her forever.

There's no going back. Whatever I've done, I can't undo it now.

Emily is ruined.

23

The next morning, Eliza scurries into the room, and one look at her face tells me what I should have already known: I'm so busted.

"His Grace's requestin' yer presence."

Even though I know I should rush out, I just groan and throw the blankets over my head. No doubt he's already put two and two together given my weird antics yesterday and Emily's sudden disappearance. He'll know I was covering for her.

"Up with ye," Eliza says, ripping the blankets off the bed. Seriously. Did she have to do that?

I cross the cold wood floors and plunk down on the stool as she pulls a dress from the armoire. It's stuffed full now. Emily has been giving me gown after gown, claiming she doesn't like the color or the piping or the hemline. Girl knows a lot about dresses—I'll say that much.

"Did you have a good day off yesterday?" I ask as she pulls on my hair.

"Yes, miss. Thank you."

"No problem. I can't believe he never gives you full days off. That's totally unacceptable, isn't it?"

"'Tis twice as many afte'noons as most otha employers. 'E's quite fair."

Wait, what? Two half days a week is *good* here?

Humph. Figures. I'm batting zero at this point. I should really stop assuming things.

Gah. Whatever. Even if I was wrong about that, too, Alex is still arrogant and sexist. There's no way I'm wrong about *that.*

Right. So, uh, back to the plan. "So, um, did you hear Emily ran away with Trent Rallsmouth yesterday?" I say casually.

In order for this plan to work, everyone needs to know about Emily's getaway. And according to Emily, the best way to do that is to let the servants spread the rumors. Eliza stops brushing my hair, her hand frozen midstroke. I wish there was a mirror in front of us. I'd love to see her expression. "They ran away together. She doesn't want to marry her betrothed."

It takes another few seconds before Eliza resumes her brushing. "Oh? Is he the gentleman who arrived last night?"

I have to bite my lip to stop the grin from crossing my face. It seems the servants really *do* gossip. I bet that's how Alex knows already. He didn't notice Emily was gone—he heard about it. Perfect.

"Yes. That was him."

"'Tis . . . quite interestin.'"

"Mhmm . . . "

She grabs a sky-blue dress with white piping along the cuffs and hemline, and I put up with her usual tugging and pulling and hair-ripping routine. I haven't thought of exactly what I'm going to say to Alex yet. I thought I'd at least have the morning to come up with a speech of sorts.

Minutes later I'm descending the stairs following Eliza, my heart hammering in my chest so hard I think it's trying to break free. I can't see him. I don't have anything rehearsed. Maybe if I'd thought ahead, maybe if I'd . . .

"Miss Rebecca Vaughn," Eliza says, as if to formally present me to Alex. I walk into some kind of parlor, trying to hold my head up high and act as if I'm not at all nervous. I half-heartedly hope Eliza will stay inside the room but she doesn't; she steps aside and lets me enter.

I walk to a high-backed brocade chair with gilded arms and legs across from the big sofa Alex is occupying and sit down. I cross my ankles and carefully spread out my skirts as if it's the most important thing in the world and requires every ounce of concentration. Victoria would be proud.

"Where is she?" His voice comes out firm, demanding.

Wow. So much for stalling. I bite my lip. "Who?"

"Do not play games," he says.

I study my hands as they wring in my lap. I can play dumb, I can postpone this, or I can just tell him. Like ripping off a Band-Aid.

"With Trent Rallsmouth," I say, peeking up at him from underneath my lashes.

His eyes fly open and he sits up straighter.

"The boy from the dance? Where?"

Oh God. He does not look happy. "The gardener's cottage on the eastern edge of Harksbury."

Alex stands like he's the incredible hulk—so quickly I'm surprised the whole sofa doesn't fly back and crash into the wall.

Oh God, this was so stupid; he's going to kill me.

Or throw me in that dungeon I'm still convinced he has . . .

"Please tell me they have a proper chaperone," he says.

I purse my lips and shake my head.

He sighs, a great drag of irritation, and crosses his arms at his chest. It makes his chest bulge with muscle, and I try to focus on the fact that he seems like he could wring my neck and not on the way he looks today.

Which, seriously, is pretty hot. His face is flushed in anger, which brings out his dark eyes . . .

Focus.

"And I suppose you encouraged this tryst?"

I stand because I can't take the way he's towering over me. "Yes," I say, once we're more level. "She can't marry Denworth. She'll be miserable. So she's run away with Trent instead. I don't care what you say; it was the right thing to do."

He takes a few slow, deep breaths and then turns away from me. I can't see his face. Which is worse, because what in God's name is he thinking right now?

"You fool," he says. It's so quiet I'm not sure I've heard him correctly.

"What?"

"You fool," he says, louder this time. There's no mistaking it. "It doesn't matter what he wants, or even what she wants. Her father has to consent!"

I stop breathing. "What?"

"She is three years from being twenty-one! Her father must sign papers consenting to the marriage!"

A sick feeling grows in the pit of my stomach and then spreads, until I start feeling shaky all over. I keep my hands at my sides and ball them into fists, so Alex can't see the way they tremble.

Why didn't Emily tell me this? How could she not know that her father has to sign something for her to be able to marry Trent?

I shake my head vigorously. "He'll agree to it. Denworth won't want her now. Not after she's been compromised. He'll break it off. And her father will have no choice." My voice comes out more desperate than I'd meant it to.

He whirls around so quickly I stumble backward on my skirts and he has to grab my arm to keep me from falling over. "You don't understand, *Rebecca.*"

Something about the way he says my name makes me want to shrink away.

"Her father is a spiteful man. He has refused to see me since my father died because he would have become the next Duke of Harskbury if it were not for my existence. Do you think a man like that answers to reason? And now she has blatantly gone against him. He'd sooner force Emily into life as a spinster than consent to the marriage."

His words ring in my ears, over and over, but I can't move or even acknowledge them.

A fatal flaw. That's what this is. A monumental, huge flaw in the plan.

I screwed up. I messed up the plan.

Not just the plan. *Emily's life.* How could I have done this to her?

But there's no going back. Only forward. This has to work. It just has to. There's got to be a way to salvage it. "But she doesn't need that when she's twenty-one? Can't they just . . . date until then?"

He shakes his head and snarls in disgust. "He is her guardian. She is legally bound to honor his wishes. If he chooses to lock her in her chambers until her twenty-first birthday, he may do so."

I think I am going to vomit.

Are Alex's lips still moving? Is he still talking?

What have I done?

Emily is the type to seek love. To crave it.

A life without it . . .

I barely make it to the chair before my legs buckle.

Alex groans and runs a hand through his unruly dark hair. "I have to fix what you've done. You'd better pray I'm able."

He strides to the door and then stops. "You'd best hope my mother doesn't hear of this until it's resolved. She has a fragile constitution. I won't have you risking her health."

I nod but I'm not sure I even heard what he said.

This is a disaster. I should have tried some other way, some way that didn't involve duping Alex and sneaking around and . . .

When I look up again, I'm alone.

Alex is gone.

In a daze, I walk into the hallway and find my way to the foyer, where the butler is standing. "Was the letter to Lord Denworth delivered this morning?"

Please say no. Please say no.

The man nods at me. "Yes. Hours ago."

"Okay," I say, barely seeing the ground in front of me.

Even if I wanted to undo things now . . . it's too late. We sent a letter to Denworth telling him what Emily was doing. Telling him she wouldn't marry him and she was giving herself to Mr. Rallsmouth. It was our failsafe, in case the servant's gossip didn't reach him.

According to Emily, the *perception* of being ruined is all it takes. Just some rumors. It won't matter if we tell him it was staged.

Denworth probably read the letter. That, coupled with the way the servants spread gossip . . . It's done. Emily is ruined.

I turn and head up the stairs toward my room, gripping the banister so I won't trip. I can barely see the steps, I'm so dizzy.

I wonder what Denworth thought when he read that letter.

I wonder what Alex is doing right now.

I wonder if this is all going to end in disaster.

24

My nightmare has officially commenced. I'm sitting in a high-backed dining room chair, wearing a stiff gown and a corset, and the only other person in the room is Victoria. Based on the way she's nonchalantly slurping her soup, she has no idea what's going on with Emily.

And I have to keep it that way.

How could I have been so stupid? How could I have missed something as important as the need for parental permission?

I bet Alex went straight to that cottage. I have no idea what's going on. It makes me long for the simplicity of a telephone. At least then I could call and see what was happening! This is pure agony, sitting here just wondering and freaking out!

Victoria asked me at the start of dinner where Emily was, and I made something up. I don't even remember what it was.

The worst dinner of my life is dragging by more slowly than the tick tock of a grandfather clock, and all I can think about is what is going on in that little cottage a few miles away. Is Alex yelling at Trent and Emily? Has Trent agreed to stick by Emily no matter what happens?

The only time I stop thinking about it is when Victoria reminds me of her ever-so-delightful presence. "Rebecca, dear, slouching is rather unbecoming," she says.

I hate myself, but I actually sit up straighter when she says that, out of pure instinct. Victoria just has that motherly vibe, like you'll immediately comply with her before you realize what you're doing. I should have slid lower in my chair, but the corset makes doing that impossible.

If I ever get the chance to travel back in time again, I'm finding the guy who invented corsets and we're going to have a serious talk.

A servant sets a big hunk of beef down in front of me. I wait and watch Victoria before picking up the same fork, holding my knife in the same hand, and cutting the meat into bite-size pieces exactly as she has done. Watching her eat is like watching a how-to video on dinner etiquette. *Simon says ...*

Part of me feels a *little* sorry for her. Her whole life is all about the proper thing to do and the rules and restrictions. How much do you want to bet it's all a façade? How much do you want to bet her obsession stems from the fact that her husband had a mistress, and all she could do was put up a good front and make everyone believe everything was perfect?

No wonder pretenses are so important to her. Her husband cheated. He fathered a child with someone else. But Victoria made sure everyone would think all was perfect in the Duchess of Harksbury's life. She's flawless, can't you tell? Not a care in the world.

I guess I shouldn't have judged her so harshly.

"The roses are in full bloom. Emily and I walked around in the garden yesterday and it smells like perfume," I say, trying to be nice.

Victoria chews on a piece of meat and stares me down. "Yes. The gardens are always beautiful this time of year. The late duke had them designed to ensure that the scent would be a constant companion to those who walk the paths."

Her late husband. She's acknowledged him. The words have fallen like cannonballs, heavy and overwhelming. I'm not sure what to say, so I just stuff another bite in my mouth and hope the moment passes.

How many courses could there be tonight? I hope only three. I simply can't handle sitting here for another four or five or six courses. All this stilted conversation is too much, and given my rep, I'll blurt out something about Emily to fill the gaps.

Victoria grips her fork so hard her knuckles turn white, as if she's realized the mistake of mentioning Alex's dad. Then she sets the fork down and wriggles her fingers. Next she sets her knife down, too, and massages her hand and wrist. Her face flashes for a moment with pain, and then she's back to picking up her fork and knife as if she hopes I didn't notice.

"Something wrong?" I ask.

"All the embroidery over the years seems to have finally gotten to me," she says. I'm kind of surprised she admitted that at all. She's Victoria the fearless. Victoria the faultless.

"What does it feel like?" I ask.

"My hand tingles at times."

"It's probably carpal tunnel."

She just stares.

I shrug. "It's a pinched nerve. Do your best to keep it straight at night. If you can get some kind of brace, it will help. After a few weeks, it should feel a bit better."

Why am I doing this? I'd prefer if her whole hand fell off.

"Thank you," she says in a soft voice. But then a second later she seems to remember we're sworn enemies. "You've an elbow on the table."

"Oh." I lean back again and set my hands in my lap.

"Why do you believe Emily should not marry Denworth?" Victoria asks. She's studying her fork in such a way that I think she might be talking to it and not me.

"Excuse me?" She doesn't know, does she? Oh God, Alex is going to be so ticked off if she found out and gets wound up about it. Here I thought she'd somehow missed all the gossip. She seems to be hanging out in bed a lot, like she's not feeling well. But if the servants came to her, or if they were in the hall and were talking too loudly . . .

"I overheard you and Emily. You believe she and Denworth don't belong together. Why, pray tell, is that?"

Oh. So she's still in the dark.

Victoria only glances upward for a moment, as if she's hoping I won't realize it's her asking the questions. Not like there's anyone else in the room. Is it really that hard for her to be nice to me?

Now I'm the one studying my fork. Do I make up some fabulous reason, some compelling argument that Victoria would understand, or do I just tell her the truth? A woman like her doesn't believe in love. How could she? She was totally into the idea of Emily marrying Denworth. Said it was her duty and left it at that.

"She deserves better."

Victoria studies me for a moment. Her face is turned upward so she has to look down her nose at me.

"Better than a baron? She had as much a chance at love with Lord Denworth as she does with any one else. Perhaps more."

What's weird is I think she believes that. She states it so simply, as if it's fact. "How can that be true? Denworth is so old."

She sets the fork down beside her plate and stares straight at me. For once in her life, her eyes aren't piercing and scary. They've softened a bit around the edges. I get a glimpse of what Victoria may have looked like twenty years ago. And I think she must have been beautiful. "The duke was nearly five and fifty when we married. I was but twenty."

"And did you love him?"

The silence in the room tells me what I need to know. Obviously not. So why is she trying to convince me otherwise? I pick at a piece of fat on the roast and wait to see if she'll admit it.

"Not at first. Not until the last three or four years."

I look up at her, surprised. Three or four years? That means . . .

That's why the old duke was hoping the baby would go away. He was reconciling with Victoria. He was probably on thin ice and hoping she'd never find out about the kid.

But why couldn't he have helped her financially? They needed that.

Victoria's hands are still and she's staring back at me. Is she actually chewing on the edge of her bottom lip? Surely she's not. Victoria is poised and perfect at all times. "I did love him. But I tried not to. For years, I tried not to. And now I think of those wasted years and I wish I could have them back."

All I can do is stare. I'd been so sure she was grumpy for no reason at all. That she just thought she was better than everyone else. But in reality she's lived the most twisted and tragic love story I've ever heard. Way worse than Shakespeare.

So she's hiding behind all her perfect etiquette and all her rules.

"There are few who fall in love, Rebecca. Even fewer who stay in love. Emily has no better idea what she wants than I did. She will marry Lord Denworth, just as I married the duke. It is to be expected."

Oh, but it's not. She has no idea what is going on just a few miles away. No idea at all. She got lucky with the old duke. She fell for him. But I refuse to believe that some fifty-one-year-old guy has as much in common with Emily as someone her own age. Someone who might already be in love with her.

"Don't you think it's Emily's choice to make?"

Victoria's voice softens a little. "It will never be her choice." And for approximately one second as she looks at me, I think

Victoria is trying to tell me that she agrees. That it *should* be Emily's choice, even if it isn't.

But then she ruins it. "Your elbow is on the table again."

I roll my eyes but I pull my elbow off the table and sit back in my chair. I guess some things never change.

25

Long after dinner is over, Alex and Emily have still not returned. He left this morning to get her. What could they possibly be doing? Emily was only supposed to be gone one night . . . and we're creeping ever closer to two.

I prowl the halls of Harksbury like a caged animal. I see the library and the study and the guest chambers and the court. I stumble into the kitchens and then three more dining halls.

I don't know what they're doing, what's taking so long, what's going on. What if something crazy has happened? What if they're like, arrested, or dead, or robbed or something? This is 1815. All sorts of crazy things could be happening.

I wonder if they went straight to her father. All three of them. God, what if he's insanely mad and wants revenge for her escapades? Alex seemed to think she was pretty much screwed.

What if I ruined her life?

What are they doing? I can't take another night of tossing and turning. I want all this to be over. I want to be home. In the twenty-first century, where stuff like this doesn't happen.

The twenty-first century. I can't believe I haven't been thinking about it more. Those first couple days, I was consumed by it. But lately I've been so busy with Emily's engagement and Alex's insults and Victoria's dinner etiquette . . . I guess I've been kind of swept up in all of it.

I have to figure out what I'm going to do. I can't just live here like it's my real life. Rebecca will be arriving in just a couple weeks.

And when she arrives, my cover will be blown and everyone will know I'm a fraud. So I have to come up with some kind of backup plan or strategy or something. But how am I really supposed to find my way back?

Maybe that makes no sense, but really, do I have any other options? If I can just focus my energies on something positive, maybe the rest will resolve itself.

For now, I'm still stuck.

At the moment, I'm somewhere in the east wing, strolling along and looking at all the paintings, a candle in one hand as the rest of the house darkens. It's mostly sceneries and landscapes hanging in this hall. Pretty rolling hills, big grassy meadows, majestic hilltops. It's not really enough to distract me, but it's interesting nonetheless.

I'm staring at a stormy sea raging against some rocky cliffs when I hear her voice. Emily. She's back.

I pick up my skirts and run down the long hall, my slippers echoing loudly on the hardwood floors.

I skid around a corner just in time to see her take the first step up toward her room. She hears me and when she turns, her eyes light up. I let out a big sigh of relief. There aren't tears streaming down her face or anything. That has to be good, right?

"Where's Alex?"

"He has gone to speak with my father." Emily purses her lips, and worry creases her brow.

I stop a few feet short, suddenly feeling like a wall has gone up between us. "Did you forget he had to give you permission? I had no idea. It doesn't work that way . . . in America."

She takes in a slow, calming breath. "I suppose in the excitement, I seem to have forgotten."

"Oh." I shrug because I can't think of anything else to do. "Did he say when he would be back?"

She nods. "In two days. It is a full day's ride to my father's estate. He will have to stop at an inn for the evening."

Wow. He's riding a full day each direction and staying at a hotel because of my interference. He cannot be happy.

"Well . . . how'd the, um, evening go? Did you enjoy yourself, at least?"

"Yes. We had a lovely meal by candlelight. He brought us a delightful picnic for dinner."

"Oh, great!" I say, with false enthusiasm.

For the first time, the conversation feels forced and

uncomfortable, like we're two strangers. Emily's never looked this worried before. There's tension in her shoulders and face, and she's not bubbling over with excitement about spending an evening with Trent.

God, I really screwed this up. If Alex doesn't succeed . . .

Eventually, Emily is going to find out she trusted a complete stranger with her life. And I betrayed her.

I hate this.

"Okay, well, um, I'm going to go to bed. I suppose we'll learn more tomorrow," I say, filled with the desire to get out of her presence before I spill everything.

She nods and heads up the stairs. I follow her. We split up at the landing, each of us climbing the steps to our own wing.

I know one thing: I am getting no sleep tonight.

The next two days crawl slowly by. All I do is think of everything that could be going wrong, everything that could be going right, and everything in between.

And in between all that, I think of *my* life.

What if I'm actually missing in the twenty-first century? What if there are entire search parties, and my mom is a total basket case, and everyone thinks I got kidnapped? It was so hard to talk her into the class trip. She'll think it's her fault.

God, she would probably have to call and talk to my dad, too. And she hates doing that.

And if I pop back up and I've been missing for a month, what am I supposed to tell them? *Oh, sorry, I took a vacation in*

1815. I got a little sidetracked with this whole arranged marriage problem. You know how that works. And I went to a few balls, and I wore corsets and stuff. Actually, the whole thing was sort of fun. So don't you worry about me! Really!

Eliza comes into my room when I'm already at the stool brushing my hair. It's got to be the first time I've beaten her to the task of waking me up and gotten out of bed on my own. I think she enjoys that part of her day the most, the way she rips off the blankets and throws open the drapes.

"'Is Grace's asked fer ye."

I freeze, the brush midstroke. "What?"

"'E wishes te see ye," she says, peeling my hand from the brush and resuming the untangling of my hair.

"He's back?"

She nods.

"Oh." I swallow. So now it's the moment of truth. Did he convince her father to consent, or is Emily's life officially ruined? Is he going to tell me that I screwed everything up and he was right?

I'm getting used to the whole process of dressing and I'm done too quickly for my liking. My walk to Alex's study is like the green mile. I wonder what he's going to say. This isn't going to be fun.

I step inside his study, but no one announces me, and he doesn't notice. So I just stare.

He's writing something. With a quill and ink. The well is sitting next to his right hand. He's so intent on whatever he's writing he keeps at it for thirty seconds before he sees me. Long enough for me to see the way he narrows his eyes when he's concentrating and the way he purses his lips.

Long enough for me to wonder what it would be like to kiss him.

Oh God, where did that come from? I hate him. Hate him. There's no way I could possibly want to kiss him.

He looks up at that instant, and I do my best to just smile right at him and not give away my thoughts.

"Please sit," he says, rising. I nod and sit down in the same fancy chair as before. The door stays open.

I sit as erect as possible, my hands in my lap, my ankles crossed beneath me. Victoria must be rubbing off on me.

Alex comes around to the front of his desk and rests on it, crossing one ankle over the other as he leans back.

"What you did was overstepping your bounds."

I clench my teeth, hard, to stop from snapping back. I have to see where he's going with this before I get angry.

"You went behind my back and orchestrated one of the most ill-planned, riskiest schemes I've ever seen. I am shocked."

"But—"

He puts his hand up to silence me. "I won't tell you what I had to do to convince her father to consent to the new arrangement. You are lucky Mr. Rallsmouth will have the means necessary to support Miss Emily, as she will not be receiving a thing from her father from here on out."

All I hear is *convince her father*. "So it worked?" A grin spreads across my features and I jump to my feet. "She's going to marry Mr. Rallsmouth?"

Alex pushes off the desk behind him and stands in front of me. "Have you not heard a word I said? You made grievous errors of judgment. You—"

"But I was right! And thanks to me, she's going to marry the love of her life!"

He's standing right in front of me, inches away. *"You were not right! You interfered and it was not your place!"*

I clench my fists as my anger flares to match his. "You think *nothing* is my place because I'm some lowly, untitled girl! But someone had to do it, and you didn't care to!"

"You should not have gotten involved!" he growls.

"You should not have forced me to!" I say, jabbing my finger into his chest. "You should have been there for her when she needed you!"

In an instant, he closes the gap between us. His lips hit mine so fast I can't even close my eyes. His hands find a place on either side of my face and pull me close, and for two-point-five seconds, I'm lost somewhere between closing my eyes and standing there, frozen. Somehow the eyes win out and I shut them, and my knees start to buckle as I press my lips into to his. I stop breathing and grip his sleeves with both hands to keep from falling straight over. His lips are warm and soft and . . .

And then I realize what's going on. *Who* I'm kissing.

You're not a lady, he'd said.

It stings as much now as it did the moment he said it. He thinks I'm unworthy.

What am I doing? I reel back and knock into the wall with

a loud crash that makes him jerk his eyes open.

"I, uh . . . " I stutter, then spin around so fast my skirts twist around my legs and I have to wait for them to swing around again before dashing out of the room.

26

What the heck was Alex doing *kissing me*? Better yet, what was I doing enjoying it? He's . . . arrogant and judgmental and elitist. He's convinced only a member of the aristocracy is worth his time. Or anyone else's, for that matter.

Gah! I'm so stupid! How could we have gone from screaming at each other to kissing?

My stomach twists in knots as I head straight to Emily's chamber. She's sitting in the large window seat overlooking the courtyard when I burst through the door. In less than three seconds, I'm plunking down across from her. "You're getting married," I say, trying to sound cheerful and normal even though everything is spinning around in my gut so fast I feel like I may actually puke.

She looks up and just stares, expressionless.

"It worked. Alex convinced your father."

She squeals and hugs me. She's beaming from ear-to-ear.

"This is wonderful!" She jumps up and does the most adorable dance, spinning around and around until her skirts look like a pinwheel. When she collapses back on the window seat, I can tell she's dizzy. "How can I ever repay you for what you've done for me?"

"Huh?" I missed whatever she just said. I'm too busy holding my fingers to my lips to calm the tingles.

My first kiss. That was my first kiss. And he's a duke. I just kissed a duke. And I didn't even see it coming. I'd always imagined this slow-motion, front porch, end-of-the-first-date sort of thing. The anticipation, the nerves. But it was just . . . sudden and unexpected. This is insane.

"Something wrong?" she says, her hazel eyes soft and expressive, as if I'm about to unload the weight of the world and she'll gladly bear it all.

"I—I don't know. I'm trying to figure out what's going on with your cousin. Everything he's done up until now . . . and then . . . I just can't figure out who he is, that's all."

She just smiles and waits, like she knows I'll continue once I figure out what I want to say.

"It's just . . . at the dance at the Pommeroy's, he tried to tell this other titled guy that I wasn't good enough to dance with. He told the guy he should dance with a *lady* instead. Like I'm not worthy or something because I'm just some commoner."

Emily furrows her brow. "That is quite unlike him. I'm sure he meant no harm."

"But it was just so pompous, and every time I think maybe

he deserves a chance or something, I think about it again and realize what a jerk he's been. Why would he tell Lord Brimmon I'm not good enough?"

Her head snaps around and she looks at me. "'Twas Lord Brimmon?"

I nod and narrow my eyes at Emily's reaction. "Why does it matter who it was?"

Emily hesitates.

"Tell me," I say.

"Brimmon's known as a rake at best and a scoundrel at worst. If Alex was trying to talk him out of dancing with you, it was for the sake of *your* reputation, not his."

My jaw drops. Could that be true? Could I have been wrong about him?

Sigh. I've gotten nothing right in 1815. Nothing. I've been judging him for that comment since the moment he made it.

"So . . . it had nothing to do with me not being good enough?"

Emily laughs. "Oh, heavens, no. You're his guest. How could *that* be true?"

"Oh . . . But then he was saying he'd dance with me because it was expected. Because I was his guest, he would do it out of duty. He acted like it was a chore."

Emily looks downright amused. "Harksbury has hosted many guests. Alex danced with precisely one of them: you."

"Oh."

I stare down at my hands and try to suppress the urge to grin, but I can't stop it. It spreads until I'm beaming.

Alex danced with me because he wanted to. Not because he had to.

Is it really possible there's more to him than I thought?

"Well now I've screwed everything up . . . " I trail off. I don't think I can admit to the botched kiss moment with Alex. "He's going to think I'm a total freak."

She furrows her brow. I don't know if she's wondering what's gone on between Alex and me, or what a freak is. "I am certain he would not think such a thing."

I wish I could believe her. But I know the truth: there's no way Alex is ever going to kiss me again.

No matter how much I want it.

27

It's only an hour later that a servant comes to my room. And when she tells me the duke has invited me out for a horseback ride, I'm flooded with the strangest mix of emotions. I can't believe that after running off like that, he still wants to hang out.

What is going on between us? And why do I want so desperately for it to be *something?* I shouldn't want anything. Not with a guy like him.

I mean, yeah, I might have been wrong about the illegitimate kid and Lord Brimmon, but the dude still thinks I don't have opinions or options because I'm a girl. He thinks I have a "place, my place" and that it's behind a guy.

And worse, I keep thinking about our kiss. The part where I bash into the wall in my haste to get away is a particular highlight on the reel I keep playing over and over again in my head.

When I walk out the back of the house and he turns to

look at me, it's impossible to fight the burn in my cheeks as he steps up beside me and the horse. I can't look at him. I'm so embarrassed I stare at the stirrup as if it will take all concentration to get my foot into it.

Is he going to say anything?

Is he going to apologize for just . . . *kissing me* like that? Maybe if he brings it up . . . Maybe if he apologizes, I can apologize too. For running off. It was so sudden all I could do was react.

But he says nothing. He just steps up beside me and gives me a boost. I'm up on the first try and feeling rather proud of myself as I situate my pretty skirts so they drape over my ankles. Until, that is, I see him swing aboard and am reminded of how graceful and easy he makes it look, even when his horse swings away from him when he's only halfway on.

We ride past the stable, and when I glance in, I see one of the stable boys showing the other how to do the robot, his arms stuck out at odd angles, his hands dangling. I have to bite the inside of my cheek to keep from laughing when I see Alex's eyebrows shoot up so high they're nearly to his hairline.

It's nice seeing him caught off-guard. I like it. It makes me want to do something totally crazy, just to see his expression.

We ride around the front of the house, past the gardens and bay windows and stately front entry, and down the long drive. Two grooms trail behind us, playing chaperone, but I've gotten used to them now. It's not so bizarre. Today Alex wants to check in on some of the tenant farmers or something.

And it's going to be such a long day. I'm so screwed. I've been squelching a ridiculous crush on him for days, and I can't deny it anymore. I actually like him. What the hay? That makes no sense. How can I like him? *Why* do I like him?

And on top of all that, I'll eventually have to tell him the truth about who I am. There's this dark cloud hanging over everything I do, the threat of the moment this world will be yanked from me because Alex and everyone else will realize I'm not Rebecca at all. How can I be so afraid of that? Why are there moments I'm hoping I can stay here for a long, long time?

The advantage of riding along the road is that we can ride beside one another. As we walk down a tree-lined dirt street, I can't help but think I'd rather be here, right now, than anywhere else in the world. It's sunny but a little cooler than our last ride, so I'm not sweating like crazy. And Alex is wearing an adorable jacket with tailcoats that flutter every time the breeze catches them.

"If you loosen your reins, she won't chew quite so heavily on the bit," Alex says, once Harksbury is out of view and we're well on our way.

I look down at my mare to see her grinding her teeth against the metal bar in her mouth. I can hear it, like nails on a chalkboard, but I'm reluctant to let go of my firm grip.

"Promise she won't do anything?"

He looks solemnly at me and nods. I like that he's not laughing at me for how scared I am right now. I ease a few inches of rein out, and the teeth grinding stops. The mare stretches her head a little, but she doesn't speed up.

Whew.

I look up at Alex to see him staring at me, his lip quirked in amusement. His eyes are sparkling with the reflection of the green canopy of leaves we're walking under. The contrast to the anger I'd seen there earlier is startling. His hands rest on the glossy mane of his gelding, his hips swaying with the elongated gait of his much-taller horse. There's not a speck of dirt on his jacket or a tiny wrinkle on his starched white cravat.

"Do you miss home?" Alex asks.

For a scary second, I think he knows. I think he's asking if I miss the twenty-first century and Starbucks and cars and electricity.

But then I realize even Rebecca is a visitor.

"Oh. Uh, yes." Are we on speaking terms now? Why does this all have to be so complicated and messy and . . . exciting?

And why is he not bringing up what happened earlier? Can't he just say *something* about it? There's no way I can mention it. No matter how close to the tip of my tongue it is, I can't get the words out.

"But are you enjoying Harksbury?"

What is he asking? If I enjoyed our kiss? If I regret the way I ran off? I stare at him for a long moment, straight into his eyes, even as my mare stops to nibble at some long grass and he's forced to pull up.

"Yes. I think it's going to be hard to leave."

He's still staring back at me when he nods. It's like there are so many more words passing between us than the ones we speak out loud. It makes me want to blurt out a lot of things I shouldn't.

I yank the little mare's head up and accidentally squeeze too hard with my ankles. She jumps forward and I have to grab the front of the saddle to stay on. I use my free hand to pull back, and she resumes an easy walk. Alex turns back to his horse.

"What will you do when you return home?" he asks.

"I, uh, I'm not sure. I feel a little differently, now. Than I did when I got here."

He nods as if he understands, but he can't possibly. I want to tell him about how Angela and the others ignored me before. I want to tell him about how intimidated I'd been, about how I was afraid to be myself. About how I bought these shoes but what I really wanted to buy was Angela's respect. I want to tell him that even though I know all that in some kind of objective way, I'd still feel awkward and clumsy in front of her. I'd still thrust those heels in her view and hope she noticed them. How can that be?

But he falls silent, and the words don't come. Maybe it's a good thing. Maybe he thinks I'm brave and smart, like Rebecca, and it would ruin everything if he knew how hard I tried and how I second-guessed every word that came out of my mouth. If he knew the real me, he wouldn't be interested at all.

God, what am I saying? He probably *isn't* interested. The kiss was probably a fluke—a heat of the moment thing. It doesn't prove he likes me.

We ride past a field of sheep, their wool shorn so they look tiny, with spindly little legs. We continue past rows of neat little crops and over a bridge and little stream that glistens with the sun. We ride over rocks worn smooth from carriage wheels. We ride for a mile in the cool shade of alder and maple trees.

Two hours later, we pause along the road, in the midst of cornfields. Alex turns his horse away from me and stares toward the crops for a long silent moment, and all I can hear is the distant sound of a cow mooing. And then he turns his horse around and heads back in the direction we came from.

"Are you supposed to . . . I don't know . . . see anyone today?"

He cocks his head to the side and smiles at me, like he knows he's been caught, but like he doesn't care. "Not entirely. There are days I simply want to ride and see the land that has been left to me. I fear I may never see it all."

"Oh."

We turn our horses and head back in the direction of Harksbury. I like the way he relaxes when we're this far away from it all. I'm starting to realize where he gets his attitude. Why he's so uptight.

The world rests on his shoulders. But out here, it's just us. A guy and a girl. Riding horses. Hanging out.

"Thank you," he says.

Huh? "For what?"

He twists his reins around in his hands for so long I think he hasn't even heard me. It's the first time I've ever seen him fidget.

The only sound is the crunching of the horses' shod hooves over compact dirt and loose rocks. "For being who you are," he says. "You don't accept anything as it is. Not if you don't agree with it. You see things the way they should be and not the way they are . . . and it makes me want to do the same."

I just stare at him. Where's Alex and who is this guy?

"I've never met a girl who . . . challenges me as you do. I find I'm seeing things differently." He exhales slowly. "I should not have raised my voice to you earlier. I am sorry."

I almost choke on my own spit. First a compliment and then an apology?

And yet his apology is for yelling. Not kissing me. So what does that mean? He's not sorry he kissed me?

Something warm spreads through me and makes it impossible not to grin. Somehow, after all those confrontations, I earned his respect. By standing up for something. For *someone.*

"Oh. Um, thanks," I say. "Does this mean you think I might know a thing or two you don't?" I smile at him and stare straight into his eyes.

Is this flirting?

"Perhaps," he smiles back at me, his eyes sparkling with amusement.

I wish this moment would last forever. But it can't.

He reaches down to run a hand over the glossy white coat of his horse with one of his doeskin-gloved hands.

Say it. Just tell him you like him.

He looks up at me, and I dart my eyes away and stare straight ahead.

I like you.

But I can't do it. The words are caught somewhere at the back of my throat.

"I believe my mother would like to host a dance in Emily's honor, to celebrate the impending marriage."

"Really? That's nice of her. I know she thought Lord Denworth was better." I look back at him again. Why can't I keep my eyes off him? Why do I want to just stare at him and smile all day?

He ignores my comment and clears his throat. He looks . . . uncomfortable? It doesn't suit him. "I'd like you to get a gown. Not one of Emily's. Your own."

I think I stop breathing. "I'm sure Emily has something suitable—"

"Emily is to receive a new gown as well," he says quickly. "You're to see the seamstress immediately."

"Oh. Um. Okay. I mean, thank you." I cough even though I don't need to, just to give me something to do so he won't see the goofy expression on my face as I cover my mouth with my free hand.

He nods and I let the conversation fall. It's got to be one of the most awkward convos I've had since my arrival, even though we're just talking about dresses.

Alex is giving me a gift. A gown. A *custom* gown. When is *that* ever going to happen again? Totally crazy.

But why is he doing this? Is this some kind of an *I like you and I'm glad we kissed* gift? But he's giving Emily one too. So it probably means nothing.

By the time we arrive at Harksbury, we've been gone for what must have been five or six hours. Alex and I ride past the front of the house and meet a groom around back. Alex hands off his reins and walks to my horse, and when I realize he's going to help me down, butterflies swarm my stomach.

I unhook my leg from the lip of the saddle so I'm facing him, and then he reaches up to my hips and helps me slide to the ground.

The result is that I'm standing closer than I'd been this morning when we kissed, with my back to the horse and my hands on his, where they rest near my waist. Am I still breathing? He's so close to me, staring down at me. Will he kiss me again?

Oh God . . . is he going to . . . ?

Am I supposed to . . . ? *Please* let this be a do-over of this morning . . . Wait, do I really want to kiss him now? What am I thinking . . . ? *Oh, just shut up and go with it . . .*

I stand on my tippy-toes and edge toward him, giving into the magnetic pull I've felt since the moment I met him. Just as I'm closing my eyes, I see him step back, and then I'm leaning into dead air. He's a few feet away before I right myself.

That was so not what was supposed to happen. He's staring at me with his lips slightly parted, something vaguely resembling worry in his eyes, and I don't want to look at him long enough to figure out what it is. Is he embarrassed? Repulsed?

My face burns. I was really going to kiss him and he just . . . backed away.

"I—" I can't even think of anything to say, so I just mumble something along the lines of *see you at dinner* and then pick up my skirts and scurry away. What a disaster. I'm such a freak! First, I run away when he tries to kiss me, and then a few hours later, I change my mind and go for it? Could I *be* anymore confused?

28

For the next several days, the servants are lost in a flurry of activity. They're beating rugs and polishing banisters, sweeping floors and washing curtains, trimming hedges and dusting paintings. And every time I think I've seen them all, I see a few more, until I think I've seen at least sixty.

Sixty. That's ridiculous. But then, Harksbury is different from the mansions back home. There are no washing machines or hot water heaters. Someone has to do everything, even haul water upstairs for the little basin I use in the morning to wash my face.

Emily and I go together to the seamstress in town. It's the first time I've seen town since the day after I arrived, and this time I manage to enjoy the scenery and look around a little more. The shops are quaint, all in a line, with windows proudly proclaiming their wares. A bakery, a butcher, a blacksmith, a hatmaker. Ladies stroll up and down the walkways, parasols in hand. Dust rises from the street as carriages roll by, their wheels squeaking.

Emily climbs down from the carriage with the help of the

servant, already lost in daydreams over her new dress. "I do wish His Grace had given us more time. I would have liked to have gone to the linen drapers in London, for they are more likely to have the latest sketches and designs, not to mention a far more varied selection of trimmings."

I nod my head, though I have no idea what she's talking about. We cross the rutted street as she continues to chatter about clothes, and head straight to the largest shop on the corner. The door is propped open, though it's still a bit stifling inside. My eyes adjust to the darkness of the wide room and I see a light-haired woman dressed all in gray approach us and sweep into a low curtsy. "Miss Thornton-Hawke, Miss Vaughn, pleased to meet you."

Emily and I curtsy back. I've mastered it by now, crossing one leg behind the other and bobbing until my skirts mushroom out a little bit and then I stand again. It seems weird, but I'm starting to like the formality. It's a show of respect, something people don't do often anymore.

She leads us past a few young ladies quietly sewing behind cute little desks, and over to a wall of fabrics, brocades and swaths of silk and satin overflowing onto the floor and pooling into a rainbow of color. "I'm afraid the selection is a bit lacking today. I am expecting a shipment of new designs from America in four days."

My mouth goes dry. "America?"

"Yes. Baron Gaverson's shipping company has obtained some of the finest silks this side of India. Or so he has told anyone who will listen."

"Wasn't your ship one of Gaverson's?" Emily asks me.

Oh God. A ship from America. One from the same company Rebecca told Emily she was arriving on.

It's her. She's coming. In four days. The day after the ball. And that's if it arrives on its regular schedule. Who knows? It could already be here.

The ticking clock just became a time bomb.

I grip the edge of a table to steady my quaking knees. Emily hasn't noticed my shock, and yet I'm sure my face must be ash-white.

The woman gestures toward the bolts of cloth again. "So, have you two any idea what you'd like?"

"Scarlet silk," Emily says without pause. "The ball is in my honor. I should like to be eye-catching."

The woman nods, looking pleased. "And you?"

I nod in agreement, my eyes unfocused.

Four days. And then what? As long as I didn't know when she was showing up, I could ignore it. I could pretend the real Rebecca would never arrive at all.

But reality just hit. Hard. I have no plan. Everything is going to explode in four days.

"Certainly you don't intend to match," the woman says.

"What?" I look up at her. They're both staring at me.

"Emily has chosen the scarlet. Do you know what color you'd like?

"Oh. Emerald," I say, without hesitation. "This one."

I don't tell her why. I don't tell her it's the exact shade of Alex's eyes.

I don't tell her what look will be in those eyes in four days, when he finds out what a traitor I am.

Oh God, what have I been doing all this time? Why did I think it was a good idea to parade around as this other girl?

I'm such a fool. Everything is about to come crashing down. They'll probably have me arrested and thrown in jail.

My life is over.

The seamstress nods. "Step up here and I shall get your measurements."

Emily gestures for me to go first, so I step onto a small pedestal and the woman sets to work, measuring my height and hips and waist. She doesn't speak; she just lifts my arms and moves my head as if I'm a horse and not a person. I suppose that's a good thing, because if she were talking to me, I wouldn't be able to hear her over the deafening roar of my heartbeat.

As the woman measures Emily, Emily instructs her on the latest styles of the season and the exact height of the desired hemline and the precise swoop of the neckline. Even though I'm hardly listening, I realize she knows *exactly* what she wants. She's in her element right now. Even under normal circumstances, I could hardly keep up.

The seamstress leads Emily over to a bay of drawers and they start going through "the trimmings," which seem to be lace and piping and buttons. I only hear half of what they're saying.

All I can do is stare at the ground as everything twists inside me. I have four days until the end of all of this.

Four days.

Moments later, we're leaving with a promise to return in a couple days for another fitting, and I have no idea what I've ordered. I think the words *surprise me* may have crossed my lips.

"You're really into fashion, aren't you?" I ask Emily as I climb back into the open-air carriage. I have to think about something else, something to keep the panic at bay. The sun beams down on us and I rest my head back and let it bathe my face in warmth.

"Oh, yes. My father made certain I was well equipped for my first season, and I discovered a passion I'd not realized before."

"You should be a seamstress."

Emily snorts. "A woman of genteel upbringing ought not to hold a profession."

I lift my head. "That sounds like something Alex would say. Are you seriously going to be happy just being a wife and that's it?"

The resolve in her face weakens.

"Who cares if you're not *supposed* to hold a profession? Fashion is obviously a passion for you. You've been gleefully dressing me since my arrival. And maybe you won't have some shop on Main Street, but why not design your friends' gowns and such?"

Her expression changes. It's one of wild hope. Oh no, what am I doing, talking her into things again?

Just as the driver is getting ready to pull away, Emily asks him to stop. And then with a grin and without explanation, she dashes back into the shop. I can only stare after her. Oh God, I've created a monster.

She returns moments later and boards the carriage. "I have instructed the seamstress as to how she should construct your gown. You shall be the first to wear one of my creations."

"Oh. Uh, thanks," I say, feeling unsure.

Somehow I think this ball is going to be the most important night of my life.

Or maybe just the *last* night of my life.

29

Despite the flurry of activity going on downstairs, my room remains silent. I spend an hour in the tub as the rose-oil scent seeps into my skin and the water turns cold. I prop my feet up on the edge, lay my head back, close my eyes, and dream that tonight will last forever.

Four weeks. I've been here four weeks.

Yesterday, back at the seamstress's, I learned that the ship from America had already been spotted from the shoreline. It's arriving right on time. Tomorrow, the real Rebecca will be here.

The lies I've heaped on Alex, Emily, and Victoria are going to come tumbling down. I don't know what to do now. Do I just hang out and wait for her to show up and reveal what a fraud I've been? Do I warn them and risk getting kicked out before I *have* to leave?

Would they kick me out? I have no money. Nowhere to go.

And that is why tonight must last forever. So the morning

won't come and I won't have to make a decision I'm not at all prepared for.

Emily wanted to get dressed together again, but I want to be alone. I'll spill it all if I have to hang out with her. I'll tell her I'm a big fat liar and her real friend is going to arrive at any moment. I'll tell her I'm not worthy of her friendship.

I haven't looked at my dress yet. It arrived in a box, now sitting on my bed.

When Eliza comes in, I reluctantly leave the now-cold water and accept the robe she hands me. I walk to the vanity and sit quietly as she yanks on my hair and rolls it—too tightly—into curlers. She powders my face but I decline any other makeup.

The corset and thin undergarments go on, and then I stand as Eliza slides my gown from the box and drapes it across her arm in a swath of sparkling emerald. My heartbeat quickens at the sight of it. This is my night. I'm going to dance with Alex. I'm going to convince him to kiss me again, and this time I'm not going to run away.

Tonight I will be Cinderella, because tomorrow I'm going to turn back into Callie and all of this will be gone. I'll be alone again, instead of eating with a duchess and flirting with a duke and breaking and rearranging engagements.

The gig'll be up.

I put my arms over my head and Eliza slips the gown on. It slides effortlessly over my hips and to the floor. I know by the look on Eliza's face that it's perfect. Her mouth forms a tiny *o* and her eyes widen. "'Tis beautiful, miss."

She goes around to the back, tightens the cords and adjusts the sleeves, and then walks to the box and pulls out two snowy-white elbow-length gloves. I slip them on, the cool silk sliding effortlessly over my skin.

I sit back down and she lets the curlers out of my hair and sets to work, gentle with the tendrils for the first time since I've been at Harksbury. It's like she knows tonight is different, like the gown showed her how important this is.

Downstairs, the buzz of the guests is building. Through the window, I hear horses being brought around to the stables. I feel so detached from everything already. I'm trying to force myself to think that tomorrow I might not be here. Not when they all know the truth. Not when Rebecca, live and in person, gets here. I know I should be thankful she hasn't arrived early or something, but all I want is for her to never show up at all.

I wonder if I even look like her. I bet if I saw her, I'd laugh that our identities were mistaken. I guess it's good that this is 1815 and photography hasn't been invented yet.

Once I'm wearing my slippers and the hum of the guests downstairs is too much to ignore, I stand. Eliza holds out a mirror, and when I see myself, I'm so stunned I freeze.

That cannot be me.

My blonde hair is a cascade of loose curls. A string of pearls weaves its way through the tendrils, like a sparkling tiara. The neckline of my gown scoops low enough to hint at the boobs I barely have, but which are currently pushed halfway to my chin and squeezed together with this corset. Humph. So maybe corsets serve a *teeny* purpose.

The long full skirts of my green dress nearly touch the floor, and the hemline is sewn with hundreds, maybe thousands, of translucent green beads. It must have taken dozens of workers to sew that many on in such a short time. The beading is mirrored along the empire waist and neckline.

Emily has done an amazing job. She really *does* have a future as a designer. It's a shame she can't be the next Donna Karan or something. But at least all of her friends, whoever they are, will be dressed in the hottest fashions.

It's sad that I can't be one of those friends. The knowledge of that tiny fact twists inside me and makes me feel hollow.

"Ye shall have te hide from Emily, else ye steal the attention."

I grin at Eliza as a shot of adrenaline courses through me. I can do this. I can stop thinking about tomorrow and just enjoy tonight.

She leaves the room, and I walk to the window and take a few deep calming breaths as I watch the grooms scurrying back and forth with guests' horses.

When I think I can handle the idea of mingling with all these strangers, I leave the sanctuary of my room and head toward the entry. The buzzing of conversations and laughter quickly escalates into a dull roar. It's a little weird, seeing so many people talking and mingling in the lobby below as servants take their jackets.

When I reach the top of the stairs, there's an odd moment when the conversations die down, and I think everyone is staring at me. No, that's me being paranoid. They're looking—

but only some of them. I smile shakily and resist the urge to smooth my skirts or check my hair, and instead let my gloved hand slide over the banister as I descend into the entry.

There seems to be a steady flow of people going in one direction, so I follow the throngs, curious as to where they're heading. And then I round a corner I've somehow never taken before and am shocked to see two of the largest doors in Harksbury propped open wide enough that I can see what's beyond them.

A ballroom. All this stinkin' time, there's been a ballroom at Harksbury. I can see, now, that it makes up one of the walls bordering the courtyard. It even has two doors. How can I not have noticed this?

The wood floors gleam underneath chandeliers filled with dancing flames. Diamonds and satin sparkle under the lights. A band fills one corner and dancers fill another. There's a table so long it stretches from one wall to another, bursting with food. Another table wraps around the corner and is filled with drinks.

Guests stream past me, and the room steadily fills.

Two women walk past, one of them bumping into me but not apologizing. They seem to be lost in conversation.

"—paid the man five thousand pounds so she could marry Mr. Rallsmouth, you know."

"The duke?"

"Yes. Apparently, her father had high ambitions for her. Wanted the girl to marry a peer. It took a bit of financial persuasion to change his mind."

What? Alex paid Emily's dad off?

I won't tell you what I had to do, he'd said.

How could I have forgotten that?

I don't know how much five thousand pounds is, but it sure sounds like a fortune.

I'm still standing in the entry, half dazed by this news, when Emily finds me. "Oh, Rebecca, you look beautiful!"

I force a smile, even though I want to burst into tears because she's called me Rebecca. We're so close now. We've been through so much. She should be calling me Callie.

I wish I could tell her, I wish I could explain, but tonight is not the time. We're celebrating. I can't ruin this night for her. But hearing her say that word is like having my lies thrown back in my face. I don't have to ask to know she's *never* lied to me. That's just not her style.

She curtsies and I take in the details of her crimson gown: scalloped hemline, cap sleeves, embroidered bust, all of it vibrant against her richly dark hair, which has been pulled up above her head with a black butterfly-shaped clip. She's a bright splash of color among the rest of the room. But the dress can hardly compete with the sparkle in her eyes; she's positively gleeful.

"Thank you," I say, and curtsy back, even though I'd rather just hug her.

"Isn't it the grandest thing you've ever seen? And all in my honor. Her Grace was quite annoyed to rush it, but we've already got our special license and wish to wed two days hence."

"You're going to be married in *two days*?"

She nods. "Yes, for there is no reason to wait when we wish it so badly."

"Cool. Er, wonderful," I say.

The ballroom is filling, but I still see no sign of the one person I want to see most. The person who commands a room like no other. What is he doing? This is his house. He's got to be under this roof somewhere, so why is he not in this room?

I need to kiss him tonight. I want to. I can't keep screwing things up and then waiting for them to magically get better for me. *Rebecca* would never do that. She'd probably march right up to him and admit that she likes him. Old Callie? She'd shrink into herself and hope everyone forgot she existed at all.

And I can't be that person anymore. Alex *sees* me. And I don't want to be invisible ever again.

"Shall we get refreshments?"

I nod to her and follow her to the array of goodies weighing down the tables. I don't even ask what any of it is; I just grab a plate and a few items and retreat. I'm used to eating mystery food now. Once I opened my eyes a bit, it turned out to be pretty good. Well, most of it anyway. Some of it's still kind of sketchy.

I don't snack for long, though. Once Alex enters the room, I forget I'm even hungry and nearly drop my plate. A helpful servant scoops it up from my hands.

I see him in profile, his long lean body in stark shades of

black and white: knee-high socks, dark, well-fitted pants, a jacket the color of midnight, and a snowy-white cravat as pressed and starched as ever. I'd think he looked entirely too formal, except my own dress is at least as fancy. Today, it's appropriate.

As much as it would be great to see him in a T-shirt, jeans, and ball cap, the formal attire simply suits him.

He surveys the room as the others take notice of his presence, but before they can bombard him, his eyes sweep across to me and then stop. His lips give way to the slightest of smiles, and then he's heading straight toward me, leaving a gaggle of disappointed faces in his wake.

"Do I look okay?" I whisper to Emily, unable to take my eyes off of him long enough to check.

She squeezes my hand. "You look . . ."

"Stunning," Alex finishes as he arrives in front of me.

"Your Grace," I say, for the first time, and curtsy.

He looks amused that I've addressed him so formally. "My lady." He bows, a deeper bow than I've ever seen him do.

I rise and look him in the eye again. "I thought you said I wasn't a lady."

He smirks. "I thought you said you were."

We smile at one another, and the room fades around me.

"Save the next dance?"

I nod.

"Wonderful. I shall find you then."

And then he leaves me with Emily, and I finally know what a *swoon* is as I grab her elbow.

"I thought he might ravish you right here on the floor," she says with a giggle.

"Emily!"

"What?"

And then I can't help it; I burst into a fit of giggles with her, until my sides ache and I can hardly breathe. A few guests stare as they pass us—I'm betting such behavior is frowned upon—but I find that I don't even care. It's been *so long* since I've had a friend who made me feel like I could be myself. Ironic, since I'm Rebecca here, but it's still invigorating and exhilarating, and all we're doing is standing here laughing like total lunatics. It's definitely against Victoria's Rules for Proper Young Ladies.

But I don't care. I am me. Whether that is someone they like or someone they despise, I am who I am, and that's the truth.

When have I *ever* been this sure of myself?

"Is everything all right?" Emily stops giggling.

"Yes. I—" I pause, taking a breath. "I'm . . . better than all right." I glance around at the beautiful, sparkling ballroom and then back at Emily's smiling face. "I'm perfect."

30

"**D**enworth is coming this way," Emily says, barely a heartbeat later.

"What? Where?"

Emily nods at an older gentleman marching toward us, and my heart leaps into my throat. He's shorter than I'd imagined, with a thin build under his colorful red jacket. His hair is a salt-and-pepper style that somehow looks aristocratic and noble. And then I look at his face.

Oh God, he looks . . .

Perfectly happy? That can't be right.

"What do we do?" I whisper, but it's too late for Emily to respond. He's six feet in front of us. Then three . . . then . . .

"Miss Thornton-Hawke," he says, bowing in front of her.

"My lord," Emily says, and curtsies. I manage to mumble the same and follow her lead. "Thank you for your attendance in support of my new engagement. I know how difficult it must be for you."

I study his face. He is older, that's for sure. Old enough to be my dad. But he has this kind sparkle to his eye. I don't feel scared or intimidated like I thought I would be if I ran into him.

"Yes, it was certainly not easy to let go of such a charming and beautiful young lady. Best wishes in your marriage."

I swallow, hard.

He's nice. As simple as that. The caricature I'd built up in my head was completely off-base. He actually wants what's best for Emily, even if he ends up getting the short end of the stick.

Emily still deserved the choice of her husband, of course, but obviously Alex wasn't trying to force her into marrying a lecher or anything, either.

And he probably knew that. If Denworth is a member of Alex's "polite society," Alex had probably met him. And knew he was a good guy.

That explains a lot.

"Thank you," she murmurs. "I hope your evening is an enjoyable one."

"Likewise," he says. Then he nods toward the two of us and walks away.

All I can do is watch him retreat. Emily wouldn't have been downright miserable with him. Would she have been in love? Unlikely. But he is not what I thought he'd be. Far from it.

"He doesn't seem upset about the broken engagement," I finally say, after a long moment of silence.

"No, he doesn't, does he?" She smiles, more to herself than to me. "I was surprised he would come, but then I think it was to squelch any further gossip. By giving his approval, he makes it appear as if it were mutual."

"Oh. That makes sense."

She nods. "And no doubt he's back in the marriage hunt."

I smile. I hope he finds someone who will make him happy. I guess he deserves that.

Before I can think of it any more, the song transitions, and butterflies swarm my stomach as if they're a mob of angry bees. I haven't even begun to search for Alex before he arrives at my elbow, escorting me toward the floor. The crowd parts as we walk through. I really am Cinderella tonight, about to dance with my prince.

We take our place in the formation, and I realize for the first time it's Victoria at the head, demonstrating a dance. She's glowing. This is her thing, this high-society hostess stuff. I've never seen her beam from ear-to-ear like this.

Whatever floats your boat, I guess.

Once the dance has been demonstrated, Alex bows to me and I curtsy, and it begins. We put our palms up to one another and walk in a small circle. I feel his eyes on me in an intense stare. It warms my cheeks.

Once back to my starting place, I drop my hand and turn in the opposite direction, and the move is repeated, palm to palm. I hate that there are gloves between us. I hate that I can't just wrap my arms around his neck and dance with my cheek against his shoulder like I would in the twenty-first century. If I had the guts, that is.

Next we move away from each other and do-si-do around

another couple. I spin twice, my skirts flying out around me. Then I return to him, on my tippy-toes, then bow away from him, and then go up on my tippy-toes again.

His eyes never leave me. He's tall enough to see over the heads of most of the other guys in the room, and as we twist and twirl and bob and bow, he never stops watching me. And instead of feeling gawky and clumsy, it gives me the strangest boost of confidence. I am flooded with adrenaline and energy. It runs up and down my arms and legs, and I want to grab his hand, gather my skirts in my free hand, and run away from the crowds so I can be with him. But I know it wouldn't be proper, and so we simply dance.

With every twist and dip, my smile grows. This must have been how Emily felt at the last dance. The reason she was glowing. And yet my brain keeps battling with my emotions, willing me to *tell him* who I am, to unload the truth. I know the clock is ticking. I know at any moment I can have everything yanked from me—yet another way I'm like Cinderella.

Every time we stand closely, every time he's looking at me, I try to tell him. I try to say *I'm not Rebecca*, try to say that I need to talk to him in private, but I can't get the words out of my mouth.

The song changes. The dance changes. But we don't leave the floor. We dance through three songs. It must be at least an hour's worth of dancing. I give up on the idea of telling him *anything* tonight. It can wait. It has waited thirty days; it can wait another. I'll find him in the morning, before Rebecca arrives. I'll explain it all.

It's not until I'm entirely too short of breath and dizzy—I

blame it on the corset—that I have to bow out. Alex tries to follow me, but he is quickly swarmed by girls in fancy dresses and thick gemstones, and I can't help but smirk at the look on his face. I'm starting to think he doesn't want to be a duke at all, even if he doesn't say it out loud.

There are whispers as I leave the floor. All eyes are on me. I need fresh air, so I leave the room and find the courtyard, where several ladies are milling about. Emily is one of them.

"I was beginning to think you'd simply keep dancing until the guests had all gone home."

I laugh. "I was a bit short of breath."

"I'm sure the young ladies in attendance thank you."

"Was it that obvious?"

"His Grace would not have noticed if the ceiling had fallen in."

I know I should be embarrassed, but I just keep grinning. "I'm sure he was just being polite."

"A single dance would have sufficed. Three means he's taken an interest. Tongues will wag. You, my dear, have just become the belle of the ball."

"Oh, I didn't mean to steal your—"

Emily laughs. "Not at all. I owe my engagement to you. You may take all the attention you want."

I smile at her and try not to notice that what she's saying is true. People are watching us.

She's so sweet not to care that I'm stealing her limelight. She's just that kind of person.

I need to say something to her. I need to make her understand that no matter what happens tomorrow, I consider her a real friend.

"Emily . . . I . . . I wanted to say goodbye to you."

She looks up at me, startled. "Oh, I know my marriage seems so very close, but we have two days yet—"

"I know. It's just . . . things are going to change soon. And I want you to know that no matter where you—or I—end up, I've treasured the last month with you. You're a true friend. And I appreciate you being there for me. I will miss you."

She smiles, her eyes glittering, and hugs me. "And I feel the same for you, Rebecca."

It's like a stab to the heart. I wish I could tell her. I wish I could explain that's not who I am, but it would ruin her special night. So I bite back the words and simply nod and fight away the tears that spring to life in my eyes. "Shall we return?"

I don't want to miss the rest of the night. I don't want to miss a single dance. Emily nods, and the two of us hook arms and walk toward the ballroom.

And that's when I hear the collective gasp as it travels through the crowd. That's when the music stops and everyone goes silent.

"*My God!*" someone says.

"Who is it?" someone else asks.

I freeze halfway through the door, paralyzed.

Oh God. There's only one thing that could be happening.

Only one reason the guests would be that stunned.

Rebecca.

She's here.

31

I rush out of the courtyard, moving at lightning speed, though I can hardly feel the ground beneath my feet. I don't know whether to flee Harksbury altogether or run straight into the fray and try to explain myself.

It's over. It's all over. Alex will know everything. Emily, my first real friend in a year, will hate me. Victoria will know she was right to snub me.

I stop when I realize no one is looking at me.

If they knew I was an imposter . . .

What are they looking at?

They're crowding around the area where all the dancers had been.

"Is she all right?" someone asks.

"She just collapsed," someone else says.

I grab the guy nearest me by the shoulder and spin him around. "What's going on?"

"Her Grace has fallen."

"Her—Victoria?"

The man nods.

I shove past him, past three young ladies in sheer, clingy gowns, and push my way into the crowd, elbowing my way past guest after guest.

"Excuse me!" I have to push, hard, to get one of the guys to back up.

Alex is on his knees beside her, and all I can see are the hem of her gown and her toes. She's lying on her back.

Oh God, oh God, oh God. This is not good.

"What happened?"

I fall to the ground beside him and pick up her wrist, trying to find a pulse. There's nothing. No, no, no! Is she dead?

"She was dancing and then said she needed to sit down. She complained of chest pain. Before she could make it to the chairs, she collapsed."

I'm leaning over her, my ear near her lips, but I hear only silence. She's not breathing.

"Was she holding her arm or flexing her hand? Her left one?"

"What?"

"Was she or not?"

"I—yes. What are you doing?"

I've started chest compressions. What if they don't work through the corset? It's so hard to tell if I'm on the right part of the sternum or not. Oh God, I hope it works anyway. If it doesn't, if she doesn't come back . . .

"One-and-two-and-three-and—"

Alex shoves me, hard, off his mother, and I land on my butt, barely managing to catch myself before knocking my head onto the ballroom floor. My elbows slam into the ground, and pain shoots up my arms.

"You're killing her!" he growls.

I swallow, slowly. "She's not breathing, Alex," I say, knowing I'm not supposed to call him that in front of guests. "She's already dead. You have to let me do this. I can save her."

There's a wild look in his eyes as he hovers over her, as if he intends to protect her from an outward force while the life is slowly disappearing on the inside.

Every second matters. What is he doing? She's dying. She's lying there dying, and he's stopping me from doing the only thing that could help.

Agonizingly slowly, he leans back on his knees. I don't wait for him to give me permission; I just leap forward and pick up CPR again.

I press my lips to Victoria's, and the crowd around me bursts into a hum of conversation. They must think this looks totally crazy. When was CPR invented? I'm sure they've never seen it before.

They must think I'm a freak.

But I don't care. She can't die. Not like this. Not now.

I give her two breaths and resume the chest compressions. "One-and-two-and-three-and-four-and-five," I chant. I concentrate on the numbers, on the rhythm, and refuse to look at anyone in the room.

She can't die. I won't let her.

This is so unfair. Her whole life, she's gotten the shaft in everything. She had a husband who cheated on her, and when he finally realized she loved him, he died. And now she lives all alone with nothing but her precious etiquette.

She can't die like this.

Two breaths.

Five more repetitions.

She's so pale. What if I'm doing this all wrong? I only learned it last year, and we used dummies.

Two breaths.

Five more repetitions.

Alex is gripping his knees so hard his knuckles are turning white. The crowd seems to be pushing closer.

"Make them back up. She needs air!"

Alex is on his feet in less than a second, pushing the crowd backward.

Two breaths.

Five more repetitions.

Did her eyelids just flutter?

No, that's the dancing candlelight. Just shadows.

Please God, don't let her die! This can't happen. She can't just disappear like this.

Two breaths.

Five more repetitions.

My lungs are screaming. I'm giving her all my breath. Or maybe I'm holding my breath. I'm getting dizzy, pushing on her chest.

"One-and-two-and—"

And then she moves. Her fingers flex and wiggle. She groans softly and I rock back and sit on my heels, watching as her eyes roll around underneath her eyelids.

And then they pop open. Her eyes are completely unfocused. She's staring upward, toward the chandeliers. She blinks a few times.

"Mother?" Alex's voice comes out garbled, like he's choking back the same lump in his throat that I feel in mine.

She's alive.

I saved her life.

I don't realize I'm crying until I feel the tears slide down my cheeks and drip to the ground.

She's alive. Thank God, she's alive.

"What . . . ?" she says in a hoarse whisper.

"Shh . . . " Alex says, holding her hand. "You fell. I thought you were gone but . . . Rebecca saved your life."

Rebecca. Of course it was Rebecca. Why am I surprised and hurt every time I hear them call me that?

Victoria turns to look at me, and her eyes bore straight into me, slicing right through my heart. "Thank you," she whispers.

I nod as I climb to my feet, feeling the oddest mixture of elation and . . . nerves. Panic? It's all hitting me now, as I stare straight into her eyes.

I just brought her back to life. I did that.

I find myself backing away from them. The room is closing in on me. I need to get away, get some air.

I flee the ballroom and head toward my chambers.

32

Hours pass. I listen as the house falls silent, until I'm sure I'm the only one awake.

I saved Victoria's life. As much as that freaked me out when it happened, I feel nothing but a sense of peace now.

I hated her when I met her, and yet when she was lying there dying, all I wanted was for her to come back and yell at me for putting my elbow on the table. Maybe I never fully understood her, but I know she's a good person. And it wasn't her time.

And yet even as dramatic as that moment was, it's not her I'm thinking of now. It's Alex.

With just a few hours left until Rebecca arrives, I have finally admitted the truth: I'm in love with him.

How could this have happened? I *just* realized I didn't hate him, and now I'm full-on falling for him? For a guy who will probably hate me when he finds out I'm a fraud? That I've scammed his whole family into believing I was someone else so I'd have a roof over my head?

I slide out from the heavy comforter and go to the armoire. I know exactly where to look, and moments later I'm pulling on my jeans and T-shirt.

The outfit feels foreign. Free and comfortable and yet *not me*. How can I be the girl who wears this? I'm the one who dances and laughs and flirts in ball gowns.

I find my Prada heels and slip them on, carefully buckling the straps.

When did these shoes get so comfortable? A month ago, walking in them was torture. And now it's like they've molded to my feet. Like I belong in them. Or maybe they belong on me.

I pick up a candle that has been left for me, even though it's been steadily burning and is now little more than a tiny nub. I slip into the hallway and walk toward the front of Harksbury, the candle casting long shadows on everything I pass. It's eerie, like the haunted mansion at Disneyland or something. I half expect to see a ghost pop out.

I descend the stairs, cross the grand foyer, and quickly leave the house. I set the candle down on the porch and cross the drive until I stand on a small patch of grass. The moon is so bright it casts shadows.

I lie down on the grass and stare up into the stars. There are millions of them, sparkling and twinkling against a velvety-blue sky. I don't look at the stars very often anymore, but I bet they look nothing like this in the twenty-first century. It seems like I could reach out and grab a handful.

The door creaks open and I sit up, sure it will be a servant asking if I've lost my mind. But it's not.

It's Alex. He stands at the entry and looks straight at me. He's not wearing a jacket or cravat, just a snowy-white shirt left loosened at the collar. It's the most relaxed I've ever seen him. For a long time, we just stare at one another. There's an invisible barrier between us, and I don't think he'll break it.

But then he does. "Might I join you?"

"By all means." I gesture to the lawn as if I'm Vanna White, and he walks over and takes a seat beside me. For a second, I think he's going to say something about my clothes. He stares for a long moment, his lips slightly parted, but then he just closes them and doesn't say a word. He's finally figured out I'm always doing the unexpected.

I lie back down and stare into the sky. "It's a beautiful view, if you lie back. If, you know, that's proper or whatever." I silently curse myself for reminding him of etiquette, because we both know this doesn't fall under Things A Duke Can Do With A Girl He's Not Married To.

He smirks, those perfectly full lips curling up on one side, but does as I say and lies down beside me. As soon as his arm brushes mine, my heart beats triple time. His fingers find mine and he interlaces them, until we're holding hands and staring upward. I fight the urge to glance at our hands to see if the moment is real. I close my eyes and lose myself in the feeling of his bare skin on mine for the first time. He brushes my finger with the pad of his thumb, little circles that make my skin tingle and jump. I can't believe all those times and all those pairs of gloves, and finally, it's just *him*.

"Did you enjoy yourself tonight?"

I open my eyes. "Yes," I say, barely above a whisper. I'm afraid to break the moment. It's too perfect.

"You looked beautiful," he says.

I smile. "You did too," I say, and then cringe. "I mean, handsome."

Silence falls over us, and all I can think are a million different ways to start a conversation in which I tell him that everything he knows about me is a lie. Every last thing.

I have to do this. I won't be able to take the look of betrayal on his face the moment Rebecca shows up. I know I could lose him this way, too, sooner than I would if I just waited for her, but it's not right. He makes such a point of being the perfect gentleman all the time. How can I keep up this charade? He deserves so much better.

"My name isn't Rebecca," I blurt out. I stare at the sky as if I'm counting every star and can't tear my eyes away from them, but I don't actually see any at all.

His hand stops moving and the silence hits me like an anvil.

He turns to look at me. And when I turn toward him, my face is so close our noses nearly brush. I'm afraid to breathe.

"Who are you?"

I close my eyes. This is too intense. I can't look at him right now. He's probably never told a lie in his life. He won't understand why I had to. "My name is Callie. I'm American, but that's probably all I have in common with Rebecca. I was lost, somehow, the day I came here. I knew no one. And then Emily came along and called me Rebecca and invited me in, and I just went along with it. Except the real Rebecca is going to show up tomorrow and everyone will know I'm just a fraud."

My eyes are still firmly shut. I can't look at him. I'm afraid of what I'll see in his eyes, afraid of what he's going to say, afraid he's going to hate me.

"Open your eyes."

And yet I can't. They're glued shut.

"Callie," he says.

I open them. Relief floods me as I see that he doesn't look angry. "Say it again," I say.

"Callie," he says again, his lips quirked in a soft smile. "I knew you weren't Rebecca the moment I met you."

Now my eyes fly wide open. "What? How?" My mind reels back to that moment in the dining room. The moment he looked at me and his eyes shifted, and I feared he knew. And then when he merely bowed and I curtsied, and he returned to his seat, I was overcome with relief, thinking he didn't recognize me as an imposter.

He did. This whole time, he knew. That's why he looked at me oddly. That's why he was so cool to me during dinner.

"She has brown eyes. Yours are blue. She also has a dimple. Emily may not remember, as she was so young then. But I do. I was quite sweet on little Rebecca. I knew the instant I saw you that you were not her."

"But you didn't say anything!"

He smirks. "To be honest, I was intrigued. I intended to question you in private, so as not to alarm my mother or Emily. But then I saw the change in my cousin. She had been quite despondent over her impending marriage—until your arrival. I admit I had no intention of interfering in her engagement, yet I could hardly take away what happiness you brought. Perhaps it was a way of alleviating my guilt for not helping her. And aside from that, you seemed to be doing no harm." He grins at that last statement, as it's obvious I was up to far more mischief than he realized.

"You mean all this time I've been freaking out over you hating me and you *knew*?"

He smiles sheepishly. It's the closest thing to embarrassment I've ever seen on his face. "Yes."

I groan. "I guess I deserve that."

I turn back to the sky, and for the first time, an odd sense of peace washes over me. I want to stay here. I know now, without a shadow of a doubt, I want to stay here. Those mixed feelings have been replaced by something else: fear. Fear that it's not really my choice to make.

His thumb picks up its soft circling on my hand. "What will you do now?"

"I don't . . . I don't know. I mean, I'm so lost I can't find my way home. And maybe that sounds weird, but it's true."

"You may stay here. As long as you need to."

I squeeze his hand. "Thank you. I'm not sure if I should, though. I belong somewhere else, and there may come a day when I need to go. When I . . . *have* to go. And I don't want you to . . . I don't want you to put anything on hold because of me."

I can't believe I just said that. I can't believe I implied

he'd be so stuck on me that he wouldn't pay attention to the other girls and his supposed duty to find a wife. A *Duchess for Harksbury*.

"I would not wish you to leave if it is not your desire."

I nod and swallow the boulder-sized lump forming in my throat. I don't know if he feels quite as strongly for me as I do for him, but he does care about me. And it feels good. "Thank you."

We turn back to the sky again, and I edge closer to him. I feel strange, dressed in my jeans and T-shirt, while he is still dressed as he always is. It makes it so painfully obvious that we're from different worlds. Worlds that will never see one another. Worlds much too far apart.

I turn toward him, so my cheek is resting on the cool grass. When he looks back at me, his eyes nearly blend with the blades until all I see is a sea of intense green.

And then I do it. I edge closer to him, close my eyes, and *kiss him*. His lips are as soft and full as before, but I enjoy it this time, because my mind isn't reeling like it was. I lose myself to the moment as he presses back against me.

It is perfect. It is everything I want it to be and more.

And then we both retreat, and I open my eyes.

He moves his arm so that it wraps around my shoulders, and I have somewhere to rest my head, and then I snuggle up against him and close my eyes again, as the heavy draw of sleep lulls me under.

33

I must have fallen asleep on a rock. It's digging into my shoulder blade. I scrunch up and start to roll over, but then freeze.

It's not just a single rock. It's a giant one. Like concrete.

I go numb as I realize what this means. It can't be . . . I ease open one eye, and then in an instant I'm sitting upright and looking around. And all I see are cars. And people in blue jeans. And street signs. And I smell smog and I hear radios crackling in the passing cabs.

I close my eyes for at least ten seconds and then open them again, but it's all still there.

The twenty-first century.

I can't stop my face from falling. I'm back. Just when I'd realized I don't want this at all, I'm back. My shopping bags are strewn around me. I'm wearing jeans. A T-shirt. My heels.

I glance back to realize the Prada shop is still a few yards behind me, just where I'd left it. I'm sitting in the exact spot I'd fallen down.

I never left at all.

I stay put for a few moments as a pounding headache fades. Alex. Emily. Even Victoria.

They were all make-believe. Some figment of my banged-up brain. That means the kiss . . . God, I made it all up! Every single thing!

I want to lie back down, close my eyes, and go back. I want horrible soup and stiff corsets and lumpy mattresses. I'll trade it all to see Alex again. To go to Emily's wedding.

A man trips on my foot and then has the nerve to glare at me, even though he basically kicked me in the shin.

Yes, I'm definitely in the twenty-first century.

I scramble to my feet and wipe the dirt off my jeans and lean over to pick up my bags. And then I notice them.

My heels. My beautiful, damaged heels. I glance over my shoulder. Yes, the Prada shop is definitely still behind me. I've gone maybe four steps from the door. Nowhere near enough to ruin the heels like this. They're scuffed, dented, and scratched.

I gather up the rest of my bags, my grin in full-force. It wasn't fake. It wasn't make-believe or a dream or anything.

It happened. As sure as the mud on the heels, it happened. There's even a dent where the front door of Harksbury bounced off the toe.

I don't know how or why or anything, but somehow, I was there. I danced with Alex and helped Emily. I played a piano for a duke and a countess, and I ate more exotic animals than I ever wanted to.

But it happened. I don't understand it; I only know that the last month was real, and it was the best of my life.

I sling the bags over my shoulder and practically skip down the block. No matter what happens next, no matter what happens *for the rest of my life*, I have something no one else will ever have. An adventure to rival Indiana Jones. A crazy month that can never be replicated.

I continue in the direction of the hotel, feeling oddly out of place and right at home at the same time. A clock chimes somewhere in the distance. I wonder if it's Big Ben.

I wonder what time it is.

"Excuse me," I say to the first woman I see. She's wearing a sundress so loud I have to squint to look at her. "What time is it?"

"Two-fifty."

I thank her and then resume my walk. Two-fifty. I wasn't out long. Probably not even a full minute. I look at my shoes again, just to be sure they're still as scuffed as ever. I love them. I love every scratch and dent and mark. They're perfect.

I walk easily to the hotel, as if the shoes were made for me. As if they're sneakers and not three-inch heels.

I miss Alex.

I wonder if he remembers me at all. If no time passed here . . . what if the same thing happened there? What if the whole month starts over?

No, I can't believe that. If I remember him, he must

remember me. Emily must be on her way to marry Trent. Victoria must be as grouchy as ever. It's simply not possible that they could all affect me so much and they wouldn't even remember me. I was there. I know it.

The hotel comes into view while I'm still thinking about it, and I slow down. Mrs. Bentley could be anywhere. I so don't need to get caught, on top of everything else.

I slip into a side door using the room key and walk up two flights of carpeted stairs, my steps muffled. They're nothing like the grand marble staircase of Harksbury.

I swipe my keycard again on the door of room 312. Once inside, I drop all my bags and head straight to the bathroom.

A shower sounds like heaven. I wonder if it's possible to run out of hot water in a hotel room.

I think I'm about to find out.

I'm sitting in a chair on the balcony, watching the traffic in the street below, when I hear a knock on my door. It echoes across the room. I stare for a long while. Some crazy, wild side of me wants it to be Alex, even though that's totally irrational.

I can't really get over losing him in an instant. He was there when I fell asleep. Gone when I woke up. I wasted a month, thinking he was a jerk, and just when I realize he's a good guy, I'm gone.

I leave the balcony and manage to tangle myself in the sheer curtains flapping in the breeze. By the time I'm at the door, someone is knocking again.

I open it and my hopes are dashed. It's Mindy. She's standing there in the same jeans and pink cami as the day I left. The same cami as *this morning.* "Hey."

"Oh. Hi," I say, one hand still on the doorknob.

"So, um . . . "

Does she look *nervous?* Is that possible?

"Me, Angie, and Summer are going to sneak into a club tonight. And, uh, I wanted to know if you're interested," Mindy says, staring at the carpet.

Oh my God. She *is* nervous. The whole time I thought she was ignoring me because I was an embarrassment. Is it possible she just didn't want to put herself out there either?

I guess we have more in common than I thought.

I'm just standing there, staring at her.

"I was going to invite you earlier, in the bathroom, but you just kind of ran off," she says.

"Oh. Uh—" I pause for a second. To be honest, room service and sleep sounds too good to pass up. Maybe a pint of Ben & Jerry's to drown my sorrows.

How could he be gone just like that? The first time I've ever felt like I was falling in love . . . and now we're two hundred years apart. Talk about a long distance relationship.

"Um, I don't know."

"Come on, you have to. When is a chance like this going to come along again?"

She has a point. A nightclub in London. It would definitely be different from that ball at Harksbury. And when this is all over, I'll be back home again. Friendless. After a month with Emily, I can't go back to that. I have a chance to change it all.

Starting with tonight.

"Okay. Sure."

Mindy grins. "Awesome. We're all getting ready in my room if you want to joins us. Room 315."

I don't tell her I already know that. "Okay. Let me grab some stuff. I'll be over in a minute."

Mindy dashes off before I can change my mind, slinking along the walls like a secret agent. I almost forgot we were supposed to be doing this all on the down-low.

I pick up the shopping bags near the door, where they've lain since I dropped them over four hours ago. I dump them on my bed and sort out the clothes. Tight hoodies, tees, tank tops.

I pick a teeny little tank top with lace across the top and pair it with new jeans. I don't even have to wonder what shoes I'll wear: it's Prada all the way. I grab my makeup case and curling iron, even though they both feel foreign in my hands, and head down the hall, barefoot.

Tonight, my life changes.

Tonight, Rebecca and Callie become one. And I'm never going back.

34

When Mindy opens the door, pop music assaults my senses. I wish it were classical. I wish it were like the band at the dance.

I wish I could dance with Alex again, silly little do-si-dos and dips and spins.

Mindy waves me in and returns to the chair near the mirrored closet door, where she's busy pinning her hair up in a dozen little twists. It's half done, but it looks cute already.

And somehow I'm not jealous.

Summer is sitting on the bed, strapping on some black stilettos. "Hey."

"Hi."

I toss my stuff down on the empty bed behind her and then stand there, wondering what I should do. The bathroom door is closed, so it's not like I can change.

"I did my makeup in that mirror. You can slide my stuff over if you want," Summer says, pointing to the little desk in the corner. Those two sentences are more words than she spoke to me our entire freshman year. I wonder if it's because Angela isn't in the room.

"Thanks." I walk over and plunk down on the chair and lean over. I look a little tired. Technically, I did stay up until nearly dawn yesterday. Or would it be this morning?

I'm only halfway through with my makeup when Angela strolls out of the bathroom in a miniskirt and backless top.

"Wow," Mindy says. I wonder if it's the same *wow* I was thinking. As in, *Wow, skanky much?* I decide not to ask.

"Oh. Hey." Angela looks at me like I'm a maid, come to fluff her pillows.

"Hi." I prop my foot up on the chair and lean in again, toward the mirror, to apply another layer of mascara. It's already a little clumpy, but I'd rather look busy than have to talk to Angela. Why do I let her do this to me? How can one second of standing in the same room reduce me to feeling completely unworthy?

"Nice knockoffs," Angela says as she descends upon the bed and pulls her legs up, even though her skirt rides up. I can see her hot-pink underwear.

I stand up and stare straight at her. "Are you talking about my *shoes*?"

"Yeah. Get 'em off a street vendor or something?"

I open my mouth to tell her that no, I did not, and I have the receipt to prove it, but then I stop. Does it really matter anymore? Do I even want her to like me? She's about as fake as the girls who follow Alex around. They drool over wealth and titles and popularity. And the second you have any of that, they're your new best friends. But they'll never, not in a million years, be *real* friends. Not like Alex and Emily.

I'm done with her. I'm done with caring about her. I'm done with letting her make me feel inferior.

"Something like that," I say, and turn back to the mirror.

I don't need her anymore. And it feels good to finally realize that.

An hour and a half later our televisions are set on low, our beds are stuffed with pillow people, and we're slipping out of a cab in front of the club. My heart pounds with adrenaline.

But I'm not scared. All the rules and etiquette and the insane social ladder of 1815 showed me I can survive anything.

Even if I'm not Rebecca anymore. It's a little like slipping off a protective mask, and I feel a bit exposed.

I tug my tank top down a little to shield the last inch of bare skin from the night breeze, and follow the three girls down an alley. This feels decidedly uncool, to be traipsing through mud puddles and squeezing past overflowing dumpsters, but whatev. It'll keep my mind off Alex.

Alex. God, I wish I could have brought him with me. Put him in a pair of jeans.

I need to stop thinking of him. Stat. It makes my chest ache.

Once we're behind the building, the sound of a heavy base beat intensifies. It's practically rattling the street. An unlabeled side door swings open and a head pokes out. I take him to be the guy who is supposed to be getting us in, because

Angela rushes over and hugs him. He's got short shaven hair, à la Justin Timberlake, and he's wearing a black T-shirt that hugs his bulging muscles. He steps aside and holds the door open for us, and then I follow the girls inside and try not to blush as he nods at me when I walk past.

It's dark, except when the lights strobe and illuminate the floor filled with dancing people. A heavy beat reverberates in my chest and makes my lungs rattle.

I follow closely behind Mindy, afraid I'll lose her if I so much as look around. We make our way through throngs of people and away from the floor, toward a mixture of eclectic seats and asymmetrical couches. Angela climbs a few steps until we're on a balcony halfway between the floor and ceiling, not up an entire story but not exactly on the main level either. It reminds me of the terrace where the band played at the Pommeroy Ball.

I don't realize until I sit down that the boy from the door has followed us, and he's got three other guys with him. I stare down at the table and pick up a paper coaster like it's the most interesting thing in the world, because suddenly the self-consciousness is coming back full force.

And then it actually *becomes* the most interesting thing in the world. A single word is embossed in fancy calligraphy letters. A single word that makes it feel like the whole room is spinning.

Harksbury. What in God's name?

"What is this?" I point at it and shout in Mindy's ear.

She scrunches her eyebrows. "A coaster?"

I groan. "No, I mean, the name. Harksbury."

"Oh. It's the name of the club. I don't know what it means, though."

I do. It's the name of a dukedom. I wonder if that means some relative of Alex's invested in this place or something. Or if someone borrowed their name. Or what. But it has to mean Harksbury is real, that it existed. I stare down at the word again. If the shoes weren't enough . . . It has to be real. And seeing it like this reminds me of how I felt there. How it felt to be Rebecca.

I tuck the coaster into my back pocket and try to ignore the stare Angela is giving me. She probably thinks I'm totally nuts, stealing a paper coaster. But it's the closest I'll get to a souvenir of my time-bending trip. And having it on me makes me feel stronger, somehow, like I can always be that girl at the ball.

I look up when the boys file in and sit down on a bright orange couch shaped like a slug. "Ladies. This is Grant, Tim, and Alex," door-boy says. He doesn't even introduce himself. I guess I'm supposed to know who he is.

I smile at Grant and nod at Tim, but when I get to Alex, I only stare.

Alex. *The* Alex.

No, no it can't be. His hair is shorter, his skin smooth and shaven. He's got on a green button-up, left open at the collar, which brings out the intense emerald shade of his eyes. There's something different. The contour of his lips, the line of his nose. It's almost him, but not quite.

And he's staring back at me. Does he know who I am? No, that's silly. It's not really him. Not Alex Thorton-Hawke, the

Duke of Harksbury. Just Alex, the twenty-first-century guy standing in front of me. In a nightclub. In real life.

Mindy jabs me with her elbow. "This is—"

"Callie," I say, standing and reaching my hand out. "My name is Callie."

It feels so good to say that. To be *me*. I grin involuntarily at the realization.

He smiles and shakes it. "Hey."

For a second neither of us says anything else. We just keep shaking hands and staring at each other. My heart hammers out of control. I feel sweaty already.

But it's adrenaline. Excitement. I'm not terrified anymore. Not of Angela, not of Alex. I can do this.

"Do you want to dance?" I ask. Did I really just say that out loud? That couldn't have been me. That was someone else.

"Huh?" He can't hear me over the music.

"Do you want to dance?" I say, louder this time, with a little more conviction. For emphasis, I nod my head toward the floor. I'm really doing this.

"Yeah." I'm not sure I've heard him correctly, but then he grabs my hand and leads me away, and I risk a glance back at the group.

They're just staring. For once in my life, I've upstaged them. I grin back and then turn my attention to Alex. I've thought about getting close to him for a month.

I'm about to get my chance.

Acknowledgements:

If I could thank only one person for making my dream come true, it would be my agent, Zoe Fishman. A lesser agent would have given up on this novel, but you never did, and I'll never forget that. This page exists because of you.

Also, many thanks to:

My writing BFF, Cyn Balog, for taking this whole crazy ride with me and sharing the tears when I got THE CALL; my real-life BFF, Rachel Stoneburner, for being there to celebrate with; Ronni Selzer, the Grammar Queen, for keeping me in line; Mindi Scott and Andrea Perrin, my Red Robin Clique, because it became real when I was with you guys; Lauren Barnholdt, because I think of you as my mentor even though you never offered; the woman who started it all by filling our bookshelves with books and sparking in me a love of literature: my mom, Donna Hogerhuis; my brothers, Danny Hogerhuis and Brian Hogerhuis; my dad, Dan Hogerhuis; the first family members ever to read my work and tell me they loved it: Nicole Kaiser and Janae Prince; Jennifer Rokes; Jennifer Lynn Barnes; Regina Scott; Sara Bennet-Wealer; everyone at The Debs, FictionPress, and LiveJournal; and the whole crew at Razorbill for their efforts in making this book the best it can be. Last, but certainly not least, thank you to my editor, Lexa Hillyer. In many ways, coming to Razorbill after such a long journey was like coming home, and I was thrilled to end up with an editor as smart and savvy as you. You know what they say: the third try's a charm.